The Cursed Planet

Liam Adams

Cover illustration by Liam Adams

The Cursed Planet

by Liam Adams

everyoneneedsaliam.com.au

We think this book is mostly suited to children from 10 years old, and young adults, 12 and over, although older adults may enjoy it as much!

This book is sold on the understanding that it is the work of a person with intellectual disability and Autism. All creativity is from the author and the text has been edited by his mother to the best of her ability. However, it is understood that the writing may be different from that expected in a formally published novel.

Liam hopes you enjoy reading his book as much as he enjoyed writing it. He would love to hear your feedback; if you wish to contact him his email address is ltahm@icloud.com

Canberra, Australia

May, 2025
ISBN: 978-0-6455970-6-6

Acknowledgement to Creative Australia

Liam was absolutely thrilled to receive a Grant from the Australian Government through **Creative Australia**, its principal arts investment and advisory body, that allowed him to write, self-publish and sell 2 new fiction books: The Cursed Planet and The Man Everyone Forgets. The grant is part of Creative Australia's **Arts and Disability Initiative**. Thanks so much to the wonderful Creative Australia!

Table of Contents

Preface 1

1. One Little Job 5

2. The Curious Letter 13

3. Finding Information in the Smallest of Places
    19

4. Meeting with the Most Dangerous Man Alive 29

5. The Impact of Arguing While Failing 40

6. A Spooktacular Forest 45

7. Spending the Night 52

8. The Loneliest Tree in the World 61

9. Fireworks! 70

10. Speaking to the Queen 77

11. The Upcoming Battle 86

12. Winner takes All 96

13. Final Preparations 102

14. Show time! 110

15. A Fresh New Start 120

Appendix 125

Liam the Author 125

Original Outline for The Cursed Planet 127

Example of Liam's unedited writing.................... 130

Liam telling his stories through cartoons 134

Preface

For some reason, this place gave Floyd an awful feeling; he wasn't sure what it was, but it gave him a strong sense which he knew wasn't normal for an ordinary planet to create, or any planet in fact. Something more was going on here, and Floyd knew that this may not be just a visit.

Greetings all fellow readers! Welcome to a spookier chapter of the Librarian Saga, and the origins of this book: the Cursed Planct!!!

THUNDER SOUND EFFECT!!!!!

The idea of this novel came to me during my work on creating all the other characters that Floyd meets in this giant series. First, we have Jack and Vicky (Papers Through the Hollows), who mostly give a supportive role that tie right to Ryan (The Lost Humans), who gives Floyd the chance to go on further adventures. Then there is Charlotte (System of Trees), which gives another character's perspective, who is like the other three before but doesn't tie right into Ryan's family. And then there is the Mercent Siblings (Gateway Into Mayhem), which I made a bunch of troublemakers who were more untamed than any other cast member that Floyd had hung around with yet.

The Cursed Planet introduces the last cast members of the saga - two really good buddies called Dez and Walls. I always admire the laid back and chilled sort of guys they are, who normally hang out and party.

It was my idea that having these types of characters would be quite fitting to put in the final cast of the saga as a whole.

The story itself was something I thought was a typical "into the woods" sort of story: a scary forest with monsters lurking around and it's not safe.

I wanted to give that sort of feeling while not going totally extreme and uncomfortable for the readers. They might like the mysteriousness and creepiness of the hypersphere, but I wasn't trying to make the story scary in the long run.

This is a book that I did plan that's entirely focussed on one planet, where the whole plot is mainly based. But I also wanted to bring a certain different element to the book which none of the previous four books have dived into, and that's the fairy tale/fantasy context. The Librarian Saga isn't really the series that goes on this road, but I wanted to add something quite enchanted about Damola and why it was so haunted.

This book gives you a much deeper understanding of Damola's whole culture and why it had become as it was now. I also mention the fantasy part as I wanted to make a Kingdom that didn't have the advantage of technology but used something else (magic!) instead. They don't have big gunners or ships but mostly plate armour and hand weapons.

I also wanted to bring a reflection of a different side of Damola, which shows that some people are isolated as they shy away from the rest, while others are found in a more protected area where they can live in harmony.

And there's the other bit.

I also wanted to add a crime boss, who also lived on Damola, whose life was full of greed, until he found something that entirely changed his perspective on the universe.

So, you get a lot of newer parts of the series: a somewhat "forest" story, a creature story and a fairy tale to wrap it all together.

When I also started writing this book, early parts and even stuff that gets left in was originally meant to tie into a future Librarian Saga book - keep your eye out for it when it drops by in the future!

So, I hope I've left you, reader, in suspense as to what is to come. Come over to the campfire, hide under any tree if necessary and delight yourself in this unusual story…

Liam Adams, Spring 2024

1. One Little Job

Somewhere drifting in deep space in the middle of nowhere, with no habitable worlds nearby, but all the glittering stars for company, a transport cargo ship was delivering some alien jugs with incredible design.

These jugs, including some other amazing other-worldly artifacts, were displayed in an exhibition on a space station for a couple of weeks, and were now on their way back to their home worlds of origin.

The ship itself wasn't a regular cargo ship by any means. A few may call it a 'special class' type which wasn't special. It was leanly as it stretched into eight carriages. Most of the museum's display was in section six with some security on board. The jugs were placed on stands in rows. The carriage interior was looking glimmer with tiles that matched the walls and floor. The security were all different types of species, and they all wore bullet-proof armour.

The ship had enough security to transport what was in the museum. They always went and checked that everything was all in order to get the objects to their destinations safely.

Everything was operating as expected, but things were about to get a shifty turn.

Nearby was a much larger and imposing ship. The comparison between the two was laughable; as you might say, a poodle was larger than a bird egg.

The larger ship drew closer to the cargo ship and hovered above them. The cargo crew had no awareness of this because for one thing, the other ship was cloaked.

One of pilots noticed the ship after one song on their radio. He looked up and saw that the ship plunged down and attached their docking clamp onto one of the carriages. As the pilot thought he should do something, he called through the speakers, "We've been invaded!!!"

Then, with the next song about to start, the heist had already begun! One of crew from the other ship hacked the cargo ship's systems and sleek invisible doors slammed down around the carriage that the jugs were in.

There were a few security officers in the room. Some prepared to protect the jugs, while the others tried to get the doors open. Then, from above the carriage, the invaders cut out a circle from the roof while using a tool that heated and burst through the metal. Sparks rang around as the men below watched.

The cargo crew were in position as they got their blasters set to stun. As the rounded roof collapsed, a blur of gas crowded the chamber. The security officers weren't able to stand but dropped unconscious.

The pilots tried to open the doors, but the controls seemed to block them out. Whoever hacked them must be a professional, but more to the fact: there had to be someone who was in their team who seemed to know their codes and must have passed them on.

Then, through the fog of smoke, four smugglers leapt down with ropes attached to their backs. They wore gas masks which covered their faces so that no one could identify them. They detached the ropes as they walked over and carefully stashed the jugs in a raggy bag. The cargo crew saw them through the door and yelled in frustration and demanded the smugglers put them back. But seeing how things were going poorly for the cargo crew, that wouldn't happen. The smugglers showed a preference for getting on the nerves of the officers and getting away with it.

The pilots did as much decoding as they could and were nearly getting somewhere. That was, of course, until the smugglers headed back to their spots where they left the ropes and attached them onto their backs again. They swung up just before the doors opened up again allowing the cargo crew to charge forward.

Then the large ship detached its docking clamps. The smugglers had one last trick left for the cargo team: they shut down the cargo ship's entire power, so the crew was stranded with no chance of chasing the thieves.

One of the two pilots watched in horror as he feared he was going to lose his job on his first shift; while the other one just watched in disapproval as the thieves got away.

"Well," he said, "that's another job gone!"

The smugglers flew light years towards the strange, mysterious and cursed planet called Damola. There have been tales, fairy tales if you like, with dark twists in them. It was once a world that had a gigantic society with millions in its population. It was full of wonder, beauty and was rumoured to be magical.

But a mysterious cursed plague turned the planet into what it is today - dreaded with sorrow, the gorgeous forest turned lifeless. No one knew what happened to its people. There was no sign or evidence or clue that they may still be alive. Rather, it seemed that they must be all extinct through this mysterious plague phenomenon.

These days, Damola was the home of the rich crime boss known as Earn Frick. Earn was old but don't underestimate him. He had many thugs and hired men under his control. Sometimes he ordered them to steal devious bounties of whatever pleased him the most. Whatever he wanted they got it for him; no matter how impossible it was to get, he got it.

Earn lived in his very own private castle in an open area that faded away from the fogs that surrounded the entire planet. His castle had massively high defences with personal guards in many different areas. Earn also had some servants around the chambers.

In the long hallway, tapestries hung upon the walls and a statue stood in the middle of a man. Two curvy stairs led up and behind the statue, and who stood above it was Earn.

He beamed at the thieves he had hired as they carried the goods, that were contained in two separate boxes on wheels. Earn gave them a pleasant smile.

"I see you have done your jobs quite well," he said quite generously.

The leader of the group nodded.

"You said it was going to be a challenge," he replied, quite smirky as he studied the boxes. "Their ship was easy to crack."

Earn was happy to hear it. He liked that the people he had recruited were worth keeping around so they could come in useful time and time again. There were also a few that had failed him and Earn had plans for them!

Earn slowly walked down the stairs to congratulate his men.

"Even though that I am pleased with what you have accomplished here today, do remind yourselves to keep your secrecy. If anyone knew about my shady deeds, if anyone knew who you were working for, remember that I won't be so complementary. There will be consequences down the track, and I will hunt for whoever speaks about it."

There was a shiver, a tension that warned the men that whatever reckoning Earn shall bring to them, he will certainly deliver that promise. Because if anyone double crossed him, or messed up big time, he wouldn't take it quite so easy.

"Yeeeess Sir," the leader bowed. "I will keep that in consideration."

"Very good. Trot along now." Earn told them as the smugglers quickly took off.

As Earn walked back into his quarters, the room was dimmed except for the overall large window that beamed shallow sunlight. In front of the window lay a desk that had many papers he had written, a bookshelf on one side of the room, and another door leading to his study. On the far corner was his bed.

In the room was Earn's top scientist, Professor Nicator, who was working on some breakthroughs. Nicator was an expert in many disciplines such as advanced technology or knowing how to sabotage a ship where they won't find any traces or evidence. He was one of the top scientists who ever lived and Earn knew that he needed Nicator's incredible ability for his own gain.

Nicator wore round glasses with pointy dark brown hair. He also wore a purple tie underneath a jacket - which did say he was a nerdy scientist - as he was working for a fearsome crime organisation.

Nicator noticed Earn enter the room. He closed the book he was reading while sitting on a comfortable chair.

"I can take it that the mission was a success?" Nicator asked Earn.

Earn stared at Nicator quite narrowly. Earn had a list of people he had trusted in the past, but that trust only went so far. Luckily, Nicator was on that list, but Earn always had his suspicions about everyone he knew.

Earn shook the look as he walked into the chamber.

"Have you made any further developments, Professor?"

"I made satellites across millions of light years in our galaxy, so if there was anything that we were keen on finding, we would be able to find it," the scientist said, as he focussed on the papers of his mathematical work.

"Very good," Earn commented, as he lay down on his bed, feeling quite drained.

Nicator turned to looked at the crime boss, who looked pale and weak. Although it was something that Nicator didn't have the right to say, he had to say it:

"If I may be so bold," he started, "we have to talk about your health."

"It is not in your area of speciality," Earn told Nicator back. "Let the doctors deal with that."

"But you should consider what you're going through," Nicator warned him. He was no doctor, but he knew the treatment that Earn was undergoing. He had the best doctors and nurses, and he asked them to do the impossible: to try to keep him alive forever even if that meant he was the last thing that lived.

"You know that there's no such thing as immortality," Nicator continued.

"No!", Earn barked weakly, "I shall live till I know everything, have everything. Don't let those thoughts cloud what I can achieve."

"But you know deep down that there's no such thing," continued Nicator, pressing the truth.

"Well, I think otherwise. Anyway, there is so much for me to focus on, what mysteries are out there that we may not be aware of. Whatever they are, I shall claim them."

2. The Curious Letter

Elsewhere, in the far future, a library, in the shape of a cube, hovered in the blackness of nothingness. The library held all the knowledge and history of humanity and everything that had ever happened in the universe before its dismal end.

The library had two robots who were busy packing some old boxes of their belongings that they didn't know was theirs. There was also the librarian who had returned after an absence. When he returned, he promised to give his robots some notice on where he would be going each time he travelled using his time travelling transmats.

The robots had a head start packing just before the librarian, Floyd, magically appeared in thin air as particles beamed around him. Floyd looked like he came back from some sort of party as flares of colour showed on his red robe.

LO-NO, the first robot, looked at the librarian and asked, "WHERE WERE YOU THE LAST FORTY-EIGHT HOURS?"

"It was the semi-finals!" Floyd explained as he took notice of the carboard boxes.

You probably think that the boxes were stored from the ceiling. But with a moveable, flying cube library drifting into the abyss, the boxes came from an area inside the library called the Honex. The location of the Honex lay underneath in one part of the library's bookshelves against a wall. Behind this wall led down to a creepy stairwell that no one knew existed. Down the bottom of the stairwell lay a wooden door that had a soiled golden nob.

After turning the nob, on the other side of the door lay giant gears that performed the functions of the library. The gears' speeds were different as some were set at the same level as each other, and some just stopped at one point, and then sometimes they moved backwards with mighty speed.

Everyone knew the builders did a magnificent job with all of this, from the details of the rooms and chambers, to making the functions work. But after you made your way across the gear platform carefully, you could find the carboard boxes on the other side, stacked up there for quite some time.

Floyd studied the boxes and asked, "What's all this?"

"AH, WE FOUND THEM IN THAT CHAMBER DOWN BELOW WHERE THE LIBRARIANS INSTRUCTED US NOT TO MEDDLE WITH."

"I think we've gone a bit overboard past meddling," the librarian commented, as he walked over to one of the boxes and opened it. The sort of items he took out were random at best. There was a bunch of notebooks - some were from the `Last Court of the Loyal Librarians'; there were some fancy displays, including a Hawaii doll and a hat – a hat that Floyd never knew existed. It was like a country hat as he observed it, but he didn't try it on.

As he scowled through the box, Floyd asked the robots, "What made you want to check out all of this random stuff?"

"WE WERE JUST CURIOUS ABOUT WHAT THEIR STORY WAS," LO-NO told the librarian. "YOU KNOW THAT THEY'VE HAVEN'T BEEN OPENED FOR CENTURIES AND EVERYONE JUST FORGOT ABOUT THEM?"

"And they've just been sitting down there all this time?" Floyd thought it was quite odd. Most peculiar. "Hmmm," he could only say.

Later Floyd's hand picked out a certain something he touched. An envelope, a really old one in fact. It had the exact red wax on it in the front that people hadn't done in a millennium.

Floyd was beaming and folded it around in different directions. Meanwhile YO-NO, the other robot, was running into the boxes as his brother yelled at him. Obviously the fixing of YO-NO's components wasn't solved yet.

Then, Floyd noticed the letter had a vague name on it, and it surprised him about what it says.

"Huh?" he said as he knew that name was not mistaken: as it was for .....Floyd.

Floyd opened up the letter and read:

Yo, Floyd, You

I know this must be really weird for you reading this, but we've met.

Sort of.

Sorry, we wish we could explain everything, but we could only write one letter.

The main thing you need to know is we're in trouble, and I mean big trouble.

And what we only know from our brief encounter, is that we need your help, and bring whatever help you have with you, we REALLY need it!

We are located on the planet, Damola.

From us, Dez and Walls

After Floyd finished this most bizarre mail he retrieved, it left him in wonder. Who was Dez and Walls? He had encountered many people through his life but no record of Dez and Walls.

And more to the point, why was the letter placed in the box, if it was for Floyd to find? He knew there were obvious explanations that Floyd could piece together, but it still left him questioning.

Whoever Dez and Walls were, they must be people that Floyd liked, and their need must be urgent. Floyd walked towards LO-NO while he was busy fighting with his twin.

"Do you know anything about this?" Floyd asked his assistants to make sure this was real.

LO-NO read the note in every syllable, and replied back, "NO"

"You sure?"

"YES, WHY?"

"Because I don't know who these guys are."

"REALLY?" LO-NO thought in amazement. "WITH ALL THE SORT OF PEOPLE YOU MEET, YOU REALLY DON'T KNOW?"

"I have a record of the people I have met," the librarian corrected his malfunctional robot. "But besides that, do you have any records of the planet known as Damola?"

LO-NO gave a curious look at the librarian as he stood there for a moment, "WHAT SECTOR IS IT IN?"

Floyd paused as he read the name of the planet and returned with an unsure impression.

"WELL THAT HELPS A LOT"

"But who are they?" the librarian asked.

It left Floyd still wondering, as it seemed that the names might have flashed in some past life, but not his. It left Floyd too many questions so he announced, "I'm going to find them!"

"RIGHT NOW?" LO-NO said shocked. "BUT WE'RE ALREADY MAKING PROGRESS!"

"They sound like they are in danger, and I have experience with getting myself around places," Floyd said, as he didn't have a clue about how bad the situation was that Dez and Walls were in. "But I think I have to go to find out the answers."

3. Finding Information in the Smallest of Places

Floyd had a trick for getting across the stars after going back in time using the transmats. There was a well-known space station called Osram Star which had been going and functioning for decades. It travelled across the entire galaxy as species from every sector came and checked it out if they weren't familiar with it.

Floyd knew that while Osram Star was a nice enough tourist destination, it was the perfect place to be if Floyd was trying to find answers and allow him to get to places quite easily.

He and LO-NO arrived at the outdoor plaza on the top where an oxygen field was surrounding the area. They could see all the stalls on either side of the pathway and the trees of the park. It never stopped amazing Floyd.

"ALRIGHT, ENOUGH WITH THE UNQIUE SCENERY AND TELL ME WHAT WE'RE DOING HERE?" LO-NO asked the librarian harshly.

The librarian gave him a hurt look while they started to walk.

"I thought Osram Star had a range of many life forms from many star sectors. I'm thinking it would likely be possible that someone on this station at least may have come from Damola."

"FLOYD", the robot responded, as he added a slight disconnection to his voice, "YOU KNOW THAT THE LAST COURT HAS AN INCREDIBLE MEMORY BANK THAT STORED AT LEAST NEARLY EVERYTHING THAT HAPPENED…".

"Get on with it, LO-NO," the librarian replied.

"I'M ONLY SAYING THAT DOES THIS PLACE EVEN EXIST?" LO-NO pointed out, "I KNOW NEARLY EVERYTHING ACROSS THE GALAXY AND BACK, INCLUDING EVERY SECTOR, PLANET, ALIEN RACE, BUT I'M NOT AWARE OF WHERE DAMOLA IS, EXCEPT IF ITS IN THE FAR REACHES."

"Well, if we can't find it through the station's resource databank, I might ask someone who may know who Dez and Walls are."

"THAT IS QUITE IMPOSSBLE MY FRIEND", the robot responded, as he knew the librarian's plan may fail. "THERE WOULD BE AT LEAST FIVE THOUSAND PEOPLE ON BOARD. I CANNOT IMAGINE YOU FINDING JUST TWO GUYS BY ASKING LESS THAN ONE PERCENT OF THE GALAXY'S POPLATION IF THEY KNOW WHO THEY ARE."

"I'm not going to ask all the people here if they've seen them," the librarian explained, "- except for some."

"THEN WHO WERE YOU THINKING WE SHOULD TALK TO?"

They shortly arrived into a restaurant which delivered the best food so most people came here to dine. An octopus faced man with a tackle beard came out of the kitchen; he gave them an unimpressed expression when Floyd walked in.

Floyd gave a waved to John with a smile as he knew his octopus friend would like that very much.

"Hi John!"

"YOU KNOW HIM?" the robot asked Floyd, as he seemed afraid to know the outcome of their relationship.

"Yeah, we've known each other for a while now," Floyd explained. "I rescued him when the planet he was on was about to be destroyed."

"AND YOU BECAME FRIENDS SINCE THEN?"

That bit jogged Floyd's memories as he did recall the relationship went differently.

Floyd looked at John who gave a careless look that said either 'Get out' or 'What can I do for you?'

Floyd paid attention to his friend as he revealed, "John, I was wondering if you may know the names of Walls or Dez? A couple of guys I've being hanging out with - or if Damola rings a bell?"

John continued to give the careless look which broke LO-NO's concentration,

"Walls or Dez? No?" Floyd asked again to get any response.

John had a bizarre and mysterious history that no one knew about, even Floyd of all people. He only spoke very briefly about his existence. The only language that he did communicate with was by eye contact.

To their surprise, John started to move as he indicated to Floyd to follow him out of the restaurant, which was something that John had never done before. Floyd and LO-NO took a moment to share glances before they lost track of John.

"IS THIS THE SORT OF THING HE NORAMLLY DOES?" LO-NO asked, confused.

"Not quite so often, no."

"THEN THAT'S DEFINITELY SUS", LO-NO remarked as they both journeyed out.

From the pace John was moving, it was casual, but he loamed with both arms dragging down as they swung back and forth. Where John was leading was through different parts of the station that Floyd had walked past but never entered.

They moved through the streets of the station until they entered a row of stairways and corridors that were dusty. The walls were tilted as the corridors became tiny and tight. Floyd imagined that no one must have travelled down here before, except for John of all people.

At this moment, LO-NO considered the people Floyd had known in his life. The ones that he forgot, the ones he wished to forget, and the others he just bumped into by accident. That last one in fact happened quite a lot.

While they marched forward in this space, LO-NO thought to drop in onto something.

"WOW! WHAT AN AMAZING DISCOVERY THIS IS TURNING OUT TO BE!"

"Trust me, I know what John is doing", Floyd promised.

"REALLY?" LO-NO replied sarcastically. "HE HASN'T SAID A SINGLE WORD SINCE WE ARRIVED HERE, AND I HAVE NO IDEA WHERE HIS TAKING US. I IMAGINE WE'LL BE OFF IN SOME SORT OF DEAD END AND WE'LL…OH, THERE WE GO."

They arrived at an entrance with a sign that was powered with a line of different light bulbs all around it. The sign said, 'Lav's Jankie Junker of Junks'.

This came as a displeasure to LO-NO as he saw it.

"UGH," he could only say. "WHY DO WE HAVE TO BE HERE AGAIN?"

"Letter," Floyd reminded him.

"AH, YES," the robot nodded as he knew he wasn't going to walk out of this one, even though it seemed to depress him that he was going along with this.

As they entered, the room had many lamps and different light bulbs from the ceiling that gave a glimmer feel. There was one part of the room's wall cut out where they gazed upon the stars, which really captured a nice view.

Besides the overall view itself, the place was a mess. Piles of scrap vehicles and robots stacked onto each other, which was hard to really not notice. There was even a massive robot head on one side of the room that had one eye missing.

The three stood on a dark red carpet that had a stylish drawing of an ancient alien culture with words of a ruined language. They came to a desk with a bell, but before they rang it, they spotted some guy with raggy clothes, including missing shoes, with an unshaved face and scruffy hair, standing on a ladder.

The man was scrolling through a tall shelf with some piles of old tech in them. He seemed to be savaging them before he became aware of their presence: he was not alone.

He soon stared down at them and called out, "helllllooooooo!!!!"

Floyd and the rest looked at him as Floyd guessed, "Lav?"

"Yes!!" he said as he jumped down from the ladder, breathing on the metal he was working on and then put it down on the desk. "I was wondering if anyone would notice my stall, but I would've thought it was too hidden to be found all the way down here."

"I WOULD SAY IT FELT LIKE A LABRIANTH, SOMETIMES," LO-NO mentioned.

"I think that makes all of us, lads", Lav agreed happily. "But welcome nevertheless. So, what may I do for ya?"

Floyd focussed on the question he was going to ask and he said, "Are you aware of the planet known as Damola, or people known as Dez and Walls?"

"Damola?" Lav replied, quite shallow as he lowered his head and took a step back and nearly hit his back on the shelf. "What sort of business do you have on Damola?"

"WE DON'T EVEN KNOW WHERE IT IS," LO-NO broke out.

Floyd gave LO-NO a relaxed stare then looked back at Lav.

"It was mentioned by the people I asked you about. They've sent me a letter and say that they are on Damola. And by what they describe, they might be in deep trouble, at least."

Lav gave them a serious glance which showed he wasn't the jolly gentleman he was earlier.

"I know someone who lives on Damola. A dangerous crime lord; a few have heard his name but have never seen him."

"What's his name?" Floyd asked as he was willing to take the chance. Hold on, was Floyd willing to risk knowing the identity of a crime lord by trying to find two guys he barely knew? This became more interesting as it went by.

"His name is Earn Frick," Lav revealed. "I've only done a few jobs for the guy but that's it. I swear to you, he is someone not to be messed with. He doesn't take it easy on anyone who's willing to see him face to face."

The tone Lav was speaking from shivered him; it made Floyd really consider what he was doing. He had the time to think it through, and later asked, "Isn't there any life on Damola, besides Frick?"

Lav gave an uncertain look. "I'm not totally aware of Damola's culture. It was always just a deserted planet with a freaky forest. No one has records of if there was a civilisation that grew from it, but mostly, it's just a ghost planet, that's all."

Nothing was ringing a bell. It made Floyd think more about it as the information drew him on. That letter had all the details to indicate that something wasn't adding up. Why was it sent to the library? It had to mean something.

At the moment, Floyd knew that he wasn't going anywhere. The traces were all leading up to there, but pieces were still missing. He had to find out if he could find a piece in his thoughts.

He asks Lav, "Can we get in touch with Frick?"

"WAIT! WHOA, WHOA, WHOA, WHOA!" LO-NO broke in, as he pushed Floyd to the side, "WHAT YOU THINK YOU'RE DOING?!"

"I've got find this out," Floyd told him, acting reasonable.

"BUT WHY? WHAT HAS IT GOT TO DO WITH US BEING INOLVED?"

"That letter, it was in the library. Why was it placed there in the first place? Who sent it?"

"THIS MIGHT BE SOME SORT OF LABRINTH TRAP," the robot thought logically. "REMEMBER THE SORT OF PEOPLE YOU'VE MET WHO WANTED YOU DEAD? MAYBE THIS COULD BE SOME TYPE OF PAYBACK THEY'RE DOING TO GET TO YOU."

Floyd shrugged as he added, "But something is different this time. Those names did remind me of someone. I don't know why but…".

"DA JA VU", the robot said.

"da ja fu?", Floyd wondered.

"IT'S A SORT OF TERM IF SOMEONE IS HAVING AN MENTAL MEMORY OR FEELING OF SOMERHING THAT THEY THINK THEY'VE ENCOUNTERED BEFORE," LO-NO looked back at Lav as he leaned closer to Floyd. "BUT FLOYD, THESE ARE SOME SERIOUSLY DANGEROUS PEOPLE WE'RE GOING TO MEET, AND I THINK THIS IS SOME REAL STUPID PLAN YOU'RE THINKING OF GOING THROUGH."

"I've got to see it to the end," Floyd told his robot assistant. "besides, you want to know what it all means."

Even as LO-NO hated to admit it, he also felt the same, as all the pieces weren't adding up. He allowed himself to tag along with Floyd till he knew the end result.

They looked back at Lav who guessed they were waiting for him to talk. "So, are you still looking for something to sell or to buy?"

"We want buy a ship," Floyd replied, "and also, we'll want to make an appointment with Mr Frick."

4. Meeting with the Most Dangerous Man Alive

They rented a Space Grover that had two moveable orbs from the back underneath the wings. It was small, white with patches of grey, and the interior was both tight and wonky. It wasn't a ship Floyd would use for a massive number of people on board.

They made their way towards Damola, which was in the Gala Region, which was controlled by the Gaol government, who were an alien race that Floyd had not met properly. They were more secretive and were quite intelligent, so it was common knowledge that Floyd hadn't encountered one of them in the flesh before.

But more to the point, Damola was so isolated that there was no history of it in any archive. Damola was one of those deserted worlds that had wildlife but nothing else, but Floyd was more intrigued about what purpose it had for his quest.

They soon flew down onto the planet's surface as they watched the forest become foggy with despair. The trees weren't dead, but they all had a creepy tilt to them, as if for some reason they were trying to scare you. Their bark was pointy, and the forest loomed on forever.

For some reason, this place gave Floyd an awful feeling; he wasn't sure what it was, but it gave him a strong sense which he knew wasn't normal for an ordinary planet to create, or any planet in fact. Something more was going on here, and Floyd knew that this may not be just a visit.

While they drifted towards their destination, they soon found a large castle which was the only part of the entire planet that shone. Nothing else lightened up except for this one spot.

They saw the castle was massive as it reached a hundred feet; and around it was a gate that had canons on the towers with many crewmen and guards zooming in every direction.

As they docked on a wide square platform with red marking outside of the castle, LO-NO took a closer look at the guards as these guys weren't anything royal with charming armour. These guys were thugs with plain black shirts, and smug and nasty looks.

LO-NO withdrew his gaze as he knew he didn't want to get into any sort of trouble, which he knew straight away Floyd was going to be a part of.

They soon entered a long hallway with a flowing trail of red carpet and windows beaming in the light. They waited as a tremor of a shiver stroke both the librarian and the robot, as they knew they were a part of something quite dangerous which might be impossible to get out of.

The minutes felt like hours as they sensed movement in every direction, but this was only their fear. They tried to not think about it, but it was hard not to.

Floyd had asked Lav to call Frick and make some excuse that they were some highly intelligent scientists. Lav was also going to tell Frick that they were going to examine technology that they had developed and so on.

Floyd wasn't bad at identifying peculiar scientific requirements and what they do, but he wasn't a professional by any means, so it took some nerve.

Then, walking slowly across the hall was Earn Frick, who spotted the inspectors in the distance. From what Floyd could see, his skin was quite pale. Frick knew he didn't look like the sort of man he was, and his body was going through a phase which didn't look well.

"Mister Frick!" Floyd called out quite joyfully, "So, do I call you Mister Frick or Earn…"

"Mister Frick will do," Earn said quite calmly, as he gave a welcome expression and tone which made the librarian relax for a bit.

The two shook hands as they meet up front.

"So I can tell that you must've come a very long way," Frick told him, as he examined Floyd with his usual red dripping robe which had the yellow and green marking that Earn wasn't familiar with. "Where are you from, if I may ask?"

To the unexpected questions, Floyd said in shock, "Berm, in the Deilrm System."

"The Deilrm System?" Earn raised an eyebrow. "Haven't I heard of that name somewhere?"

"Oh, yes sir!" Floyd replied. "It has a horde of worlds that have been overtaken by the Tale's Empire."

"Ah, yes. Near to the System of Trees I take it?"

"Yes sir," agreed Floyd.

"Hmm," Earn studied the librarian carefully as he tried not to interrogate Floyd any further. "So, what's your name?"

"Gail," the librarian lied, "and this is my bot, ZO-Seven."

"IT'S A PLEASURE TO MEET YOU", LO-NO replied as he tried to act casual, which, to all robotic experts' surprise, was hard to do.

"Ah, don't be so tense my friends," Earn told them, as he had seen their stress before. "I only want you both to feel at home; I don't want to make you feel uncomfortable."

"Oh," Floyd said, as he relaxed his muscles. "Well then, it's just that we haven't been…to a forest before."

"WHAT?" LO-NO broke out but later zipped it and continued to act casual.

Earn nodded as he made a slight smile. "I see," he spoke.

"Well, you see," Floyd explained, "we're only city and space station people. Trees and plants are entirely new to us. I haven't seen one in the flesh and I wasn't sure how we'll…".

"Its okay, its okay," Earn told him, still having the pleasing look. Floyd could tell Earn wasn't going to kill them at first glance, since he knew that they must be equals. "I've heard that you are into some of our experimental designs?"

"Yes, I am," Floyd said, not lying for the first time, as he always had a passion for someone's scientific creativity, which interested him.

"Good, because I've got something to show you and your bot," the crime boss said as they started to walk down the hall.

"I'M NOT A…WHATEVER," LO-NO said quietly.

Earn gave Floyd and LO-NO a bit of a detour as they journeyed through the castle. A few rooms were locked and kept secret as only Earn had clearance for him and other staff members who were allowed to enter.

They soon entered into a stone walled laboratory chamber. It had a number of scientists there who likely had a history of being kidnapped so they could work for Frick. The many scientists were busy working. Most of them worked in groups and some chatted around the big computer terminals.

But what Floyd took notice of, as he zoomed in the room, was that a few of them were working on different types of inventions, including one that had a big round spinning machinery.

It got Floyd fascinated but he didn't know what they were doing. He looked at one thing, then at another thing next to him, as he got distracted by everything around him.

Earn looked at him closely, and he noticed that this Gail was some type of baboon. But he also seemed quite excited at the same time.

"I'm happy that you like what you see around here?" Earn asked Floyd.

Floyd was lost in concentration as he replied, "Yeah, you sure do have quite a fascinating collection!"

"Well, thanks to these brilliant minds who can make something quite impossible possible," Earn said as the scientists stood straight and looked at him. Floyd noticed that this was against their will.

Floyd stared at them with tension as he slowly popped the question, "So…why have them here?"

Earn looked at the inspector as if he thought that if anyone did question him, there would be some type of threat. But as he already examined Gail and seemed to like him already, he thought he should just give a bit of slack.

"Oh, just to help me to scale up the defences around the castle, pouring out some visible gas around the area, and other things that keeps where we are stable."

Floyd knew that Earn wasn't giving out all the details he had with the scientists, but he thought to not bring it up again. "Well, I imagine that you got everything all sorted here so there shouldn't be anything to be worrying about."

Earn made a small chuckle as he shook his head, "Well, you would be surprised."

"What do you mean?" Floyd said by mistake.

Earn beamed at him in the eye, as he shortly answered, "The planet has a ruined history, something that every society doesn't experience. It's a fairy tale really, but I presume that you don't believe in real magic or forces of evil looming in shadows."

Floyd didn't know what Earn was talking about. Was he talking about Damola? If he was, he still didn't know what he was getting at.

Then, Earn stared over at a giant metal cage ball that was attached to two wires with separate pillars. He looked at Floyd again and asked, "Do you see that there?"

Floyd turned to face it as he replied, "Yeah?"

"I hope your fine with bright lights", Earn warned, as the scientists flicked on a couple of buttons on their computers and the room went dark except for the ball.

Then, dark blue electricity flickered across the ball as it brightened with a glow. Then after a couple of seconds, they could see within the ball was some type of projection of an entirely different galaxy unlike theirs. Floyd couldn't describe what he was seeing, the colour of the image changed rapidly as it was beyond their visual processing. Then after a couple more seconds, it started to fade away as the lighting of the room went back to normal.

It made Floyd's jaw dropped with amazement, "What was all that?!" he asked disbelief.

"What you saw, was a glimpse between many external planes that's off our reality," Earn explained. "And we were seeing the cosmos through the reflection of the mirror it has shown us."

Floyd didn't know what that meant but it seemed to really excite him. "Cool," he thought.

Then Earn decided to move onto another topic with him. "So, tell me why you are really here?" he asked the librarian. Earn was planning to distract him to get a straight answer. "I can easily tell that you haven't come all the way to Damola just to see what we do here. I've studied how you reacted, and I can tell there's something about you Gail."

Floyd returned an awkward but also quite shivery smile. LO-NO couldn't help but sense the tension within the two of them.

"Well, you see…," Floyd said as he thought he should be honest. "We are looking for two individuals that we have heard are on this planet."

"Individuals?" Earn said, quite surprised, but also quite suspicious, because if there was anyone else on this planet, he would've known. "As you are very aware, Damola has no other form of life or society. May I ask, who exactly are you looking for?"

Earn raised an eyebrow and Floyd knew he was squeezing him into another corner for an answer. Yet again, Floyd thought he should let it out before things got ugly. "Dez and Walls?" he said, "Do those names ring a bell?"

The names were unfamiliar, but also seemed fascinating to Earn, as it sounded like he might not be the only one on this planet.

"No," he spoke quite motionless. Then another question struck him, "What are they to you?"

Floyd returned with a bland and unknown expression, "I'm not sure really."

"Huh."

"But I'm guessing if you knew their names, maybe it might give me a trace to their whereabouts."

When Floyd said the word 'trace', Earn quickly made a slight glance to Professor Nicator who started scanning Floyd through the castle's monitors unnoticed.

Then Earn asked, "And what are you planning to gain from this?"

"Find answers I guess," Floyd replied, as he knew that's what the main goal was.

"Well, I'm sorry that I don't have anything to share with you," Earn expressed his apology.

"That's cool," Floyd told him to not sweat.

Earn nodded once again, "Well, I'm happy that you planned to come to visit."

"And thank you for inviting us and giving us your hospitality".

"It was my pleasure."

As Floyd and LO-NO took their leave, exiting the door from the laboratory, Floyd turned around and shouted, "And thanks for the awesome light show!" before LO-NO could shush him as the doors shut.

After they've left, Earn went to Nicator to find out if Gail had said who he really is. Nicator was really good on identifying people, knowing if they were who they say were or not. The way the technology worked here, he could do it in a matter of seconds.

Earn went beside him and faced the computer Nicator was working on, "So, who is he?" Earn asked curiously. "Some sort of agent or spy?"

The professor wasn't too sure. He knew he hadn't failed Earn on anything, but something was off. The data that the computer was giving him didn't make sense and was entirely random. But what he could make out was this:

"You may never believe this, sir, but the computer says it couldn't pick up his state of origins or ID."

"What?" Earn said quite shocked. "So he must've hacked our whole system down, as there must be someone here who has done that."

"But wait!" the professor went on further." What the computer also says is that he isn't named Gail, but someone known as Floyd. And - get this - by the reading it could calculate – he is from a completely different time. From the far future."

"The future?" Earn exclaimed. This totally changed his thought of the man he met five minutes ago; it somewhat surprised him but also gave him an urge of fascination and want. The man of the future, who travelled back in time just to see him. And with that, Earn knew that there was going to be a big bounty happening very shortly.

5. The Impact of Arguing While Failing

After they left the laboratory and returned to the Space Grover, LO-NO was growing a little more worried as he sensed that Earn must be onto them. It used to be impossible for a robot to feel this way, but things did change for him to learn how to feel and adapt.

But never the less, the robot was feeling a bit uncomfortable about being here; every minute that passed he felt that they must have triggered something on Frick's radar.

The robot waited in the piloting room where he could spot a few of Frick's men outside as they stared at him. LO-NO tried not to pay attention to them and he tried very hard to act normal, like an ordinary robot. He kept moving his seat as he tried to get the right angle.

Then soon after, Floyd was in the room and they were ready for take-off. LO-NO broke in, "TAKE OFF, TAKE OFF, TAKE OFF, TAKE OFF, TAKE OFF, TAKE OFF!!!!"

"We will, we will", Floyd told him to calm down as he was setting the engines to "On". The Grover took off from the ground and it drifted into the sky. They were hundreds of feet away from where the castle was. Floyd looked back at LO-NO who wasn't pleased, but Floyd thought he should try to spark up his mood.

"At least it was no problem."

"NO PROBLEM?!" LO-NO sparked "I SAW THOSE SCENTINISTS LOOKING AT ME AND THEY WERE THINKING ABOUT STEALING MY PARTS!"

"Don't worry about it," Floyd settled, "we're on Damola, we're going to find out who Dez and Walls are…"

"AND HOPEFULLY TO UNDERSTAND WHAT HAPPENED TO THE PLACE," LO-NO mentioned, which still left them in mystery, and they still hadn't solved any of their answers.

"And hey, maybe we may get something out of it."

"I DON'T SEE WHAT I GET."

Then, Floyd noticed on the scanners that something was flying towards them, which wasn't any sort of vehicle.

"Uh, I think Mr Frick has sent us a 'thank you present'," Floyd said, not joking.

"WHAT?!" LO-NO cried out in horror, "THEN GET US OUT OF HERE!!"

Floyd flew the ship towards the clouds while the incoming torpedo followed their trail as it seemed to get a full lock on. They continued flying above before their ship's systems seemed to be shutting down.

Floyd and LO-NO were flicking the switches of buttons where everything was down.

"WHAT SORT OF TRICK IS THIS?!"

"I'm not sure!" Floyd replied back as he continued to flicker. "They're not doing anything!"

"WELL, DO SOMETHING THAT DOES WORK QUICKLY!!"

"Nothing's working!"

"WELL, THAT'S TYPICAL!"

Then, the incoming blast hit the two orbs of the engines as the ship dropped down hundreds of feet towards the enchanted forest. Floyd and LO-NO screamed as zooming air noises passed them. They might have also heard some birds on the way.

As the ship continued falling, LO-NO added, "THIS WAS YOUR FAULT!!! WHY DID YOU HAVE TO BE SO COMPLIMENTARY ON HIS LIGHT SHOW?!!!"

"I can't help it!" Floyd called back.

"OH YEAAAAAAHHHHH???!!!!!!!!"

The ship came closer to the foggy forest as they brushed through the spikey and spooky trees as branches broke off and snapped, leaving heavy damage on the Space Grover. They soon crash landed onto the surface. They saw they were about to hit a tall boulder; they screamed louder as they braced for impact.

The crash wasn't as bad as they thought, luckily. They survived with no injuries, even though it could've ended much worse.

As Floyd and LO-NO got out of the unrepaired ship, they took in an awareness of the forest they were in. It was cold with a shiver; the sky was dark which was more greenish than rather clear.

Nothing felt pleasant being here; everything was in despair, and also a tingle of fear. The trees bent, spikey as they saw before but here they grew in every direction.

The ship was parked against a row of wide rocks that were near a gap between the trees. The two observed the area. While they knew this place was trying to scare them - and they had never been to a spooky forest before - but nothing really came over them.

But what they did feel was that they were not out of the woods yet, and chances of escaping might be impossible.

Floyd turned to LO-NO, and asked, "Where should we go?"

"ME?! WHY ARE YOU ASKING ME WITH YOUR QUESTIONS?!" LO-NO said back.

"Yeah. Fair enough." Floyd thought, as he knew there weren't really any clear signs. They were fugitives on the planet, with one powerful man, seeming to want them dead, and with nowhere to go. Where else to go? That was right in front of them.

Floyd though of an idea. "If we journey forward, we can make camp and continue on our search."

"YOU THINK THAT THESE GUYS ARE LYING IN THIS NIGHTMARE?!" LO-NO told the librarian. He looked at the forest and he knew there was no way anyone could chill here. "LOOK, I DON'T WANT TO GET YOUR HOPES UP, BUT THIS PLACE LOOKS UNLIVEABLE! HOW DO YOU THINK…"

"Listen!" Floyd shushes LO-NO. He thought he could hear some rattle on the other side of the forest, and also thought he saw something. It snuck through his senses, but he knew something was there a moment ago.

LO-NO seemed pretty lost on what Floyd was doing, but he thought to interrupt. "WELL, I'M GOING TO GO EXPLORING IF YOU WANT TO COME ALONG?"

As LO-NO was taking the lead, Floyd beamed down to the grass and kneeled down to study it. The grass was dimmed and lifeless, like every part of its soul was gone. Whatever happened here didn't seem right to him, and Floyd knew right way that he was going to find out what.

6. A Spooktacular Forest

Floyd and LO-NO wandered through the dreaded and enchanted forest for an hour and every direction they went in looked identical. The fog was getting worse as they could only see ten feet ahead. There was also no sign of any detail that alerted them about where they were going. The closest thing they encountered were small frogs and other small wildlife.

Floyd and LO-NO were both getting exhausted and confused about their whereabouts. They couldn't map where to go and were having difficulties re-tracing their steps.

"THIS FOG ANNOYS ME!", the robot called in fury. "HOW CAN WE TELL IF WE'VE BEEN THERE AND HERE BEFORE?!"

"I don't know," Floyd commented as he was studying the environment. "I can tell that there's much more to this planet than what everyone is thinking."

LO-NO looked towards Floyd, quite focused, "WHAT ARE YOU GETTING AT?"

Floyd froze for a moment as he recollected all the knowledge so far that everyone had told them about Damola. He knew that everyone said that this world had no civilisation but was just a ghost planet. It was also in the Gala Region which must have taken a recording on their radar.

But there was this weird fog that had been catching the librarian's attention, and the trees seemed to curve unnaturally. And Floyd hadn't got to the strangest part of it.

The whole area around Earn's castle was sunny and bright, separate from the frightening part of the forest. And the grass was quite damp and seemed sick in a spiritual sense.

Floyd couldn't work out any of it, but he had to comes to terms with whatever they had got involved in. They were part of the events now.

"Something is slapping us right in the face," he could only say, "and I'm not saying it literally, I'm saying that something really bad has happened here."

"MISTER FRICK?"

"No, I don't think Frick could do this much damage."

It shocked Floyd to see the place like this, as this was something entirely out of his understanding.

"It appears that this whole planet was dissolved, possibly whatever made this place was stripped away."

"BUT SURELY YOU CANNOT SAY THAT THIS…THIS IS LIKE MAGIC, RIGHT?" LO-NO bluffed, as he knew he didn't believe in such a thing. But he knew that was maybe what Floyd was getting at.

Then, Floyd and LO-NO stopped in their tracks as they spotted something growling behind them. As they turned around, they saw a creature, standing on four legs and a long snout. It wore black and white fur of some kind with glowing white eyes. It drawled with its fangs showing as they appeared to be fearsome.

Once again, something quite unnatural was with this creature; it didn't feel normal, like magic was consuming its thoughts and energy.

Then, out of the fog came one, two, three, no, five creatures that were both growling and staring at them. A sudden chill tingled within Floyd and LO-NO as they stood in terror and sweat started to consume them.

They stood for few moments until they had the urge to run. They sprinted and the creatures followed their trail keeping the same pace as them. The creatures ran with the fog as they hid in shadow, but Floyd and LO-NO could still hear their panting and footsteps.

The two collided with upcoming trees blocking their path, which they pushed through to avoid them. Soon they heard sharp barking as the creatures drew nearer. They later slid down slopes of hills and barks of wood. They snapped and broke but nothing was stopping them from journeying on.

Still running for a couple of miles, Floyd looked at one direction of the forest and noticed they weren't getting rid of the creatures. Yet again, this also triggered Floyd's thoughts that there was something strange about them.

"WE'RE NOT LOSING THEM!!!!" LO-NO cried out.

"Well, it beats Spin Cans any day!!" Floyd thought. Then they couldn't believe their chances - more creatures burst towards them. A few led in packs through short cuts in the forest, and multiple howls grew louder around them.

"GREAT, GREAT, GREAT, GREAT, GREAT, GREAT, GREAT, GREAT!!!!" LO-NO said repeatedly.

"We need to get over to an empty space!" Floyd instructed the robot.

"WHAT HELP WILL THAT DO?!"

"Something I hope!!!"

They moved deeper into the forest as the trees loamed closer and the slopes and hills faded away. As they kept running, they noticed that they had no sight of the creatures but could hear them many feet behind.

They looked to find somewhere to lay low, but everything was too much the same and if there was something to hide from, it wouldn't do any good. The howling and the sounds of small footsteps grew closer.

Then a couple feet later, in an open space, they could see a dimmed orange light, which caught their attention right away as panic filled their minds.

"Hey!", Floyd called to LO-NO, "you see that?"

The robot overserved what the librarian was getting at until he answered, "YOU WANT US TO GO INTO THAT WEIRD GLOWING SPACE?".

"Where else is there to go????!

LO-NO didn't complain as the two of them headed over to the light.

As they approached the light, they noticed it was a lamp that was connected to a pole where a strange metal hatch was next to it as it shank into the grassy surface.

"IS THIS YOUR GREAT PLAN?", the robot commented, "WE'RE GOING TO DIE NEAR TO A DITCH?"

"Just help me with this!" Floyd barked as he and LO-NO twisted the wheel. The wheel itself was incredibly tight and was hard to open.

As they continued their struggle, they could hear the creatures near ahead and they only had moments now.

Then as they finally got the hatch open, they could see a ladder leading them down. But before they could get in, they heard the barks of the creatures as they ran towards them.

Then the librarian and the robot crawled down the ladder as something yanked them just in time – a man with silver skin leapt up on the ladder and shielded the hatch.

As the panter of the creatures died off, they made a howl which sounded like they were returning back into the woods.

After such an extreme experience, Floyd and LO-NO observed the room they were in.

They were in a wide cosy living room and a kitchen next to it. The living room had piles of carpets; the walls and roof were underground dirt and nothing much stood out from that detail. And to their surprise, a TV was placed on one side of the area.

Then, Floyd and LO-NO met the people in the area. There were two gentlemen with silver skin, one of whom had saved Floyd and LO-NO.

One of the gentlemen was in his fifties and had a black beard with a cape. The other one was younger and was in his thirties at best, and he had slim black hair.

The two gentlemen held weapons in their hands. The bearded one had a long spear as the other was holding a kitchen knife.

"Who are you?!" the bearded one questioned the intruders. "Why have you come to our sanctuary?!"

But before Floyd could come up with an excuse, two young human blokes came out as they protested.

One had purple hair with headphones and wore a long-sleeved t-shirt; and the other had curly light brown hair and a colourful shirt that zinged.

"Whoa, guys! Fellas!" said the trippy one. "I don't know if you know but this is the guy we've been telling you about."

Then, it struck Floyd right away as he looked at the two of them, and he said out loud, "Dez? Walls?"

"Yes!" said the purple haired one. "Dude, we were wondering when you would show up!"

"You got the letter, right?" Floyd nodded. "Then we have everything all under control."

Dez and Walls slapped their hands as LO-NO interrupted.

"SORRY TO GET IN THE WAY OF THINGS, BUT CAN ANYONE TELL US WHAT IS HAPPENING HERE?!"

Everyone looked at each other as the two gentlemen who were threatening them before were acting much calmer as they dropped their weapons.

Then Walls mentioned, "Yeahhhh, we can get you up to speed."

"Totally," Dez nodded.

7. Spending the Night

Then finally, the answers that Floyd had been waiting for were revealed! Well, sort of. Dez and Walls explained that they met Floyd at some beach party on the planet Levith where Floyd was getting into some trouble with a group of robots that weren't LO-NO or YO-NO but said they wanted him dead. A few hours later, after finding a solution to the robots, they said Floyd spent his time partying with Dez and Walls and said he would see them again.

After they finished their story, Floyd thought it seemed quite accurate. He guessed this might have involved some time travel, possibly to give them some message or other. But overall, something still wasn't right about all this which kept the librarian in awe.

But whatever he did must have been important. Whenever he looked at or heard them, he knew that he recognised them, including their names, so it couldn't be clearer that they were telling the truth.

But the letter in the library - he knew that they wrote it but how did it end up there?

Then, while he was starting to get to know who Dez and Walls were, he met the two gentlemen that were standing in the background for this entire time.

They cut into their conversation as the bearded one said, "Sorry to spoil the moment, but who are you?"

With the tone of his voice, it sounded like Walls and Dez had not told these guys the full story.

Floyd explained, "Honestly, I'm not really sure how I fit with all of this."

The two men looked at Floyd with a curious glance. "So you really don't know," the bearded one said quite surprised but with a bit of humour. He lent out a hand to Floyd. "My name is Julius, and this is William." William nodded to welcome the librarian. "From what we have heard, you must have come a long way to get here."

"WE REALLY DIDN'T," LO-NO said honestly.

"Well, it isn't safe out in the night," Julius warned, "- or ever, in fact."

Everyone heard the cries of howling outside, and they were aware that there were still many creatures out in the wild. Then, Floyd asked, "What are they?"

"We don't have a name for them", William explained, "but most of us called them Ranges."

"'US?', SO YOU'RE SAYING THAT THERE'S MORE OF YOU HERE?" LO-NO asked.

"There's a few that we know of that are scattered across Damola," William explained, "but mostly we all went into hiding."

Julius raised a glance at William, then to the others. "Time for questions to be answered shortly; but first you should rest up."

Julius, William and even LO-NO dived across the room as Floyd was left with the two dudes that he only just met. But still, there was a lot more for him to be asking about.

During the many hours of doing not much other than catching up with Dez and Walls, Floyd noticed that the nights on Damola lasted longer: Damola had a history of staying dark.

While killing time, Dez and Walls told Floyd they were once party planners and they got some gigs being DJs. They played bits of their remixes to Floyd in the meantime which Floyd thought was…illuminating.

Then during one part of the night, William asked them to go up and check the surface to see if there was Ranges about and if they hadn't damaged anything important. Floyd climbed up the ladder as he listened carefully to see if there was any creature in sight.

"Anything?" Walls asked him.

Floyd only heard the wind and few noises of crickets and owls, but he couldn't hear anything else other than that. "No", he replied. Floyd waited for a few more seconds to make sure, as he knew part of himself wasn't ready to go out.

"Trust us," Dez enlightened the librarian, "those hatches are stronger that they look, and the Ranges wouldn't be able to open it."

"And they give up easily too," Walls added.

"Right, right," Floyd thought as he took a deep breath.

A few more seconds passed, as Dez asked, "Now?"

"Now."

"We're pretty sure nothing's there."

"Right."

"You are sure there's nothing there?" Walls asked Dez.

"I'm going…," Floyd rushed up and banged his head on the hatch, "Ow!"

Later, they made it up as the hatch opened. They popped their heads out and looked around the area and listened to see if anything was nearby.

They noticed the lamp was knocked on the ground where Floyd picked it up and studied it. As the three stood about, Floyd asked Dez and Walls, "So, how did you two end up here? It was hard enough to find it but why here?"

Dez and Walls gave a look, then Walls explained, "We were about to make our way to organize a party, you see. As we needed to hopefully pull out the biggest one the galaxy has ever seen!"

"We were just passing across the Gala System while our ship's engines were acting up and we came crashing down." Dez continued, as he made a whooshing sound effect like they were falling.

"And then we met Julius, William."

"They didn't like us very much; they thought we were pretty annoying."

Then, they were aware of how long they were staying out as they knew the risk they were taking.

"William says we only have just a few minutes to stay out here," Dez instructed.

"How does he know that?" Floyd asked curiously.

"He is a Range Listener," Walls explained. "One time, we and William came out and he studied carefully how long it took till the Ranges sensed us."

"Uh," Floyd thought as he decided, "I presume that we should head down now?"

"Right, you're probably right," Dez agreed.

"Dop!" Walls replied as they headed down and closed the hatch again.

Soon afterwards, they all sat at the dinner table in a different room. It still had the dug in underground walls like the living room but every time they noticed it made it weird.

During these many hours, Walls and Dez made Floyd welcome, while LO-NO was feeling he was at home. Julius and William thought that it should be the time to reveal Damola's forgotten history.

Floyd sat at the front of the table with Dez and Walls right beside him as Julius sat on the other side. William was serving their late dinner, Minic Pie. A sour and strange taste for a meal, but they did warn that their supplies were growing stale.

As everyone got ready, Julius coughed as he told the story of Damola, the Cursed Planet.

"Many years ago, the world was once was truly beautiful. The forest was divine and peaceful, with many creatures and animals living in harmony. Damola had a massive population, and its people knew the forest, and they sensed its aura."

As Floyd was listening to this, he knew there was a time where tree life forms communicated to trees, but something about this was different as Julius went along.

"The people studied the aura as their queen thought to place a magical seed that they created that would allow them to speak with the trees." Then Julius's expression went dim. "But that was a mistake."

"As they placed the seed, the forest started to have some side effects. The entire planet lost its spark, and its light was faded away alongside the trees dying out. Then came the Ranges which spawned from the newly evolved forest which you see here."

"People ran, hid in the hatches for shelter, but none of us ever leave our post. For the rest, they returned to the Kingdom of Larne. We have no idea the state everyone is in, but Damola has never returned its light again."

It got Floyd curious as to how they created a seed and how it made a heavy impact. "So, what was the seed?" he asked.

"Magic! Totally beyond our understanding!" Dez replied dramatically.

"We've collected many rare ingredients to formally make it," William explained.

"Witchcraft too!!!" Walls butted in.

"CAN YOU GIVE IT A REST?" LO-NO told them as this whole thing was getting on his nerves. "THERE'S NO SUCH THING AS MAGIC! THERE CAN'T BE!"

"Yeah, they say that the human race believes in gods firing lighting and creating water," Floyd pointed out, recalling Greek mythology. This wasn't going to win his companion's thoughts.

"BUT THEY'RE SAYING LIKE MAGIC IS REAL! YOU'RE NOT SERIOUSLY BUYING IT?!"

"Believe it or not believe it, they have been going through a lot." Floyd mused.

"But you will help us, won't you?", Julius asked, and his tone sounded almost like a plea. Floyd wasn't cut out to be a heroic figure; he didn't represent that. Sure, he had done things that needed some correction, but he wasn't the one that should solve everyone's problems. But he remembered what he had been through already to get here, and knowing what Dez and Walls said about needing his help, he couldn't just turn his back now.

"Well, it isn't in my role to do whatever you're asking me to do, but while we're here, I think we could at least lend a hand." Floyd told them.

"And you can count on us too," Walls added.

Good: mission was accomplished for the most part, Floyd thought. The next objective he was thinking was to work out their next action.

"So, does anyone know what we are doing?"

"We've been stranded here for a couple of days," Dez explained, "and all these guys have been here forever. They have nowhere to go and they know it is hopeless to leave."

"Except, we may have a chance," William thought with a smile.

"Damola spins around for thirty-eight hours, and we only get sunlight very briefly for a few hours." Julius explained. "We're planning on moving at the first sight of light."

"We've done all the packing tonight, so we won't waste time on our journey."

"OKAY, BUT DO YOU KNOW WHERE WE ARE GOING?" LO-NO asked.

"The Kingdom," Julius said. "We all have to start somewhere, but with the six of us, may boost our chances of getting there."

"Cool," Floyd thought, as he noticed everyone around the table were getting up. "So, uh, if there's anything I can do, I'm here."

"We'll let you know, Floyd," Walls patted him on the back.

"Yeah!" Dez commented as he showed an impression of support.

As everyone exited, LO-NO came walking up to Floyd. He thought to add something to him.

"YOU KNOW VERY WELL THAT THIS IS A BAD IDEA."

"Yeah, well, there's the option for you to go back to the library," Floyd told his robot.

LO-NO deeply agreed. He wasn't cut out for one of Floyd's adventures. He wasn't made for it, plus, by everything he had been through, he can't stand it. But he had fears that what Floyd had been through on this trail and the upcoming danger the librarian was going to get himself involved in, he couldn't sit out this one.

"NOT A CHANCE," he said as he left the room.

8. The Loneliest Tree in the World

It took a few hours more till the slightest dawn rose. It was still dark as the forest couldn't share any traces of sunlight. After they were all sorted and William gave them the sign to leave, Julius and his fellow survivors began their journey to the Kingdom of Larne.

William was wearing a leather chest plate and everyone thought he might have joined an army.

Julius and William tried to map out where the city was located. It was very difficult to find it, because it could literally be anywhere and there wasn't any sign of its whereabouts. But during the many years they spent in a hatch, they pinpointed spots on old maps that were rumoured to show where the legendary city was located.

They traced pathways and directions as they sniffed and looked where they were going. The fog still was a problem as they continued finding their way.

Much later, they arrived at a ruined village, where old buildings were burnt down or mostly as you call it, torn down.

During this detour, as Julius and William were finding their surroundings, Dez picked up in the dirt something that looked like some sort of sparkly round helmet with horns. "Look!!" he called to Walls as he passed it over.

Walls knew that he had no intention to wear a hat that had horns on it. He knew the two Damolas were too busy, the robot was too mean, but Floyd on the other hand…

He held it up as he tossed it towards Floyd. "Is that for me?" Floyd asked.

"Well, if you like hats with pointy stuff on it," Walls informed.

Floyd looked at the helmet again and thought, "Yeah, why not?"

Walls put the helmet on Floyd's head which impressed both Walls and Dez immediately.

"Whoa!!!" Walls thought.

"You looked sick!" Dez commented.

"Sick? Me?" Floyd thought, as he didn't think the hat looked that cool on him. Floyd never had a taste for wearing battle armour; he thought it would be pointless as he had a standard job as a librarian.

"Yeah, man!" Walls replied quite confidently.

"Floyd! The mightiest slayer of whatever fearsome creature approaches him!" Dez said quite dramatically.

Floyd felt some encouragement as he said that. They were giving the librarian some confidence inside him somewhere. Floyd did know that he was no warrior or soldier. He was just a guy, a guy in a silly hat.

While they were doing that, LO-NO looked at them in disbelief, as he rolled his head.

Earn Frick was fascinated about this man that he met a couple of hours ago, a man from the future who just appeared right at his doorstep. During this time, he only ate, slept, took notes from the scientists and asked one of them about where they placed one of their tubes for his secret project.

Earn returned to the laboratory where Professor Nicator worked all night and found the identity of the stranger. If you wanted to study someone who wasn't born yet and who was going to be born in the next million years, you need about eighteen brains to help you there. Nicator had one, and he was the best scientist in the castle as he could analyse anything.

"So, the person that just came here yesterday is called Floyd, who is a member of the Last Court of the Librarians," Nicator explained brilliantly. "It says that he is the last remaining survivor of mankind, with no expectations for any more life."

"How interesting," Earn only replied as he scratched his chin. A bit of this should have put him off as Floyd was the last human, but Frick had some ideas in mind. He wanted him, more badly than anything he had so far forced his men to get. He also knew that if he had

Floyd, he had all the answers he would want, and he himself would be the last of mankind.

Then, Nicator had to ask, as Earn hadn't given word about this yet. "So what is your take on this?", he asked. "Assassination? Kidnap?"

Earn shook his head.

"No", he replied. "I want to send all my men to bring him to me. Then we shall question him, and hopefully he'll cooperate and give me the secrets of how to travel to the future."

"Sounds intriguing," the professor thought.

"But then, he'll be a special trophy, staying here with no escape."

"Like a prisoner?"

Then, Earn froze. "Just think of it as an award. He has a lot to look forward to here, even though he has no freedom, but I don't think he'll have any choice in the matter."

Earn was lost in thought as his mouth opened, "Last of humanity. I think mister Floyd will be mistaken that he won't be the last!"

As the group left the small, ruined village, they came around to another part of the forest where they found a peculiar tree. It was bent, light weight and seemed pretty normal, but something strange was within this tree. Floyd, Dez and Walls stared at it as they couldn't make it out.

In fact, the true origins were that the tree was once a man who was cursed by a witch. He had wanted her to make him rich and cool, but instead she turned him into a tree. The tree was unimpressed as he looked at the three strangers looking at him,

"Is it me or is there something about this tree?" Floyd asked curiously.

Dez and Walls gave a closer look. "Nah, I think it's just a regular tree."

No, I'm not! The tree thought as it tried to reach out to them.

"You think anything happened to it?" Dez asked.

"Like it got hit by an ice cream cone?" Floyd thought.

"Something like that," Walls agreed.

No, you idiots, I've been cursed! The tree said to itself exasperated.

They stood there a while, watching it as they waited for any thought, connection or movement with this tree. But trees can't do that, trees are trees.

Then the attention caught Floyd. "I want a nice ice cream cone when we get there."

"I hope they sell the best stuff!" Dez added as they walked away.

No, wait, come back! Aww, man, how am I ever going to get out of this mess? Maybe those dears might help out. Hey guys! Its me! The tree!

They continued moving forward and finding few directions, but as every hour went by, they knew that they only had a little time left before the light disappeared.

They later arrived in a wide area where a deserted old coffee cart was parked. It was in a bad condition after standing there for all these years. A cup of coffee sat on a log as the smell of it drifted in the air. It appeared that someone made it not so long ago.

Julius sniffed at it as he passed it over to William. "I think it's okay to drink."

As William sniffed at it, he remembered the old taste of the milkiness, the dark coffee, everything that was so good to drink then. He had never tasted coffee in the last eleven years.

Then, Dez said surprised, "But why should we stop? Aren't we on a clock here?"

"And what about the Ranges?" William added.

"We'll make shelter soon enough," Julius told them wisely, "we have only got a few miles to go, then we may have some last leads before we finally reach the kingdom.”

“BUT IT TOOK US ALMOST EIGHT HOURS SINCE WE LEFT,” LO-NO pointed out as he wasn’t cut out for long walks. “SHOULDN’T WE FIND SOMEWHERE NEARBY TO STAY?”

“There should be hatches near ahead”, Julius told them as he had a strong sense he would be right. “I would be surprised if there wouldn’t be one. They’re not so far ahead from one another than what you may think.”

Then, Floyd took notice of the coffee as William drank it. “Uh…Julius? What kind of coffee is that?”

Julius turned around as he noticed what the type of coffee William was drinking. “William stop!”

William dropped the cup in horror as he collapsed on the grass. His mind drifted away as his vision became wiry and strange. He was thinking to himself how selfish that was.

“Oh…that was not good,” he said softly to himself.

Everyone stood there hopelessly, as Walls asked, “Does anyone know first aid?!”

Everyone looked at him as they said nothing, “Nobody?!”

Then a number of howls grew near the forest; everyone noticed where it was coming from and they knew that they were running out of time.

"Uh, Ranges," Floyd said in a struggle. "Uh, this is a problem."

Everyone looked at every direction as they tried to locate where the howls were coming from.

"Okay, where should we go?" Dez asked cluelessly.

"I don't know!" Walls mentioned as he broke into panic.

Floyd looked at LO-NO who gave him an unpleasant sign that they were about to die.

But Floyd knew straight away that no one was going to take charge, so it was all up to him.

"Alright!" Floyd said, "we have to find shelter now. I need someone to stay here with William while the rest of us can go and find someone who could help us."

"What?!" they all cried.

"You're not serious!" Julius told the librarian as he knew he would break the rhythm. "We'll all die if we separate from each other!"

"YEAH, BUT YOUR BUDDY HERE IS IN NO CONDITION", LO-NO pointed out. "IF WE DRAG HIM WITH US, HE MAY SLOW US DOWN."

Julius knew this was an awful plan, but as much as he hated it, the robot was right. William may not be able to move and they don't know how bad that coffee was: he had to let these strangers go.

Julius gave an unpleasant sigh as he looked straight at Floyd, "Alright, I shall stay here with him."

"So will I," Dez volunteered.

The howls were getting louder, and they thought they needed to get on the move.

"Cool," Floyd said as he, LO-NO and Walls were starting to walk. "We'll be back as soon as we can. And don't split up!"

Then, they were out of sight as they stormed into the forest.

9. Fireworks!

Floyd, LO-NO and Walls raced further into the forest as they searched for any nearby hatch. They were begging to find anyone near ahead, to find any signs or resources that may led them to someone.

But with luck, they found a woman in a dress on the other side of the forest. She was doing something with a sign that said: 'Frayn's tool shop of nowhere, where anyone could grab a thing and go away'.

She looked at the running people coming at her and feared the worse.

"No, no, no, no!" she told them off. "You're not coming in!" She stopped what she was doing and started climbing down the hatch.

"Wait!" Floyd tried to reason with her, but she didn't pay any attention.

"We've got a very sick friend who we fear is about to die!" Walls spoke out.

LO-NO gave him a nudge in the guts, as a sign of 'Don't be a jerk.'

"Isn't there like anything you could give out at least…", Floyd paused as he and the others beamed down in the interior of the hatch as it was way more different than the one they knew so well.

The chamber was full of fireworks and boxes of powder, lots of them. In fact a few dropped on the floor which made it much messier. Besides that, everything else was totally abandoned and empty.

"Are…are these fireworks?!" Walls asked as they dropped their jaws.

"And explosives," the woman called from somewhere in the basement.

"WHHHHATTT?!?!" the three said quite dramatically.

"Where's the bed?! Where's the kitchen?! Where's the people?! Is there even an emergency room?!" Walls asked, as he knew there had to be one of each thing, or it would be impossible for anyone to stand staying somewhere with so much stuff but nothing interesting to add.

"Okay, listen up!" the lady warned them as she took some thin tool out of her pocket. It was small, lean and black. As she held it up she threatened them, "I want all of you to get out of here before someone gets hurt!"

Then suddenly, a white spark flickered from the object, and as it flickered onto one of the powder boxes, her expression went shallow, "Ooooh…".

The tree wanted to lure the wildlife towards him as he tried to use some telepathy in any sort of way, trying to seek any type of freedom he could grab. He spotted a few birds that hovered and landed on a branch of another tree.

Come on, the tree tried to call out, just a little bit further. I don't have all day if you must know. I have a life, a wonderful life that must not be wasted! Now, get down here!

The birds flew away as a horde of Ranges came rushing as they started to scratch the tree. They normally do this every once and while as they go and scratch any tree in their territory. This tree, however, was one of them.

Oh, not you! The tree thought. Go scratch some other tree!

Floyd and the others watched as the smoke filled the air as the hatch was busted. The lady watched in shock and looked dusty from the blast.

Floyd and the gang knew it was bad enough to waste any more time here as they didn't want to know what the lady may do to them next. But time was of the essence. So they made their way back to where they came from and hoped nothing awful had happened after they left.

They could still hear the incoming Ranges as they were growing louder, and footsteps could be heard in the distance. By now, Julius was growing nervous as his plan was working so well until it just happened to fall apart. He hated that these outsiders didn't understand the situation that they were in. He was about to reach the conclusion that their away team may be dead.

"This is hopeless!" he commented roughly as he stared at Dez. "This is all your fault! If you hadn't brought them along, we wouldn't be in this mess!"

"Chill out, dude!" Dez told him off. "We were only trying to help!"

"But we're one down, the rest are gone and presumed dead, and I'm stuck with you!"

"Me?! What's wrong with me?!", Dez said quite hurt.

Julius didn't reply as he didn't know why he had them in the first place, "You slow down and keep bickering with all of your nonsense which I don't understand a thing!"

But before the argument grew more tense, a voice called out through the forest which got their attention.

"Guys!"

The two gazed out to see who was there, but they only saw some movement and noticed that the voice was Walls. "This way!!"

The two didn't hesitate. They got up, as Julius dragged William in his arms and they ran towards the others. Not so far away, a band of Ranges got their scent and followed their trail.

They passed through branches of trees as the Ranges kept up with them. The Ranges snuck through the branches and beamed at them through the holes.

Julius was having some difficulties carrying William as he was heavier than him. Dez came over to give a hand and Dez asked, "Have you found somewhere?"

"We did! Till everything blew up!" Walls told him the full details.

"Dude," Dez commented shocked. "way to go!"

"CAN YOU TWO STOP SAYING THAT. WE GOT COMPANY BEHIND US!!!!", LO-NO replied.

They kept running as they saw that the Ranges were all around them. A line of trees hovered above them; many appeared, and a few got in their way. They all managed to squeeze through as they saw the Ranges were trying to get through towards them. Nips and bites missed them as they got through and ran off.

They continued making way as they noticed that the Ranges were left behind. Then, they saw something on the other side, which shined with bright light. A massive citadel, that glowed in the distance. They saw a massive, tall tower in the centre with a huge gate barricade around it.

"the…Kingdom," Julius said speechless.

"YOU HEAR THAT?! WE'RE HERE?!" LONO called, as he hit a tree and fell down. He later got up and caught up with the others.

They sprinted towards the gate as the forest faded away within a mile. As they got closer to the city, the environment at once shined properly as it didn't have the enchanted effect from the forest.

The gate walls were about a hundred feet tall. They reached the gate's door, which was oak and was about the half of the size of the wall. The door slowly opened as an army awaited them.

All the soldiers had metal armour with shiny helmets. They wielded spears that were neatly shaped like a triton. There were about twenty of them in the entrance as they pointed their weapons at the outsiders.

"State your names!" one of the guards instructed.

Floyd and his pals slowly put their hands up as they didn't want to make any fast movement.

Julius, the bravest of all of them took a step forward with William still under, "This one is in bad condition," he explained.

The soldiers studied William who seemed worse for wear. The guard told one of his men, "Take him," and they took him away as the soldiers and Julius drifted inside.

Then the guard studied the rest. "Who are you? You are not Dercans."

"IS IT THAT HARD TO TELL?" LO-NO thought, as they were talking to a robotic form of life.

"We are not from around here," Dez explained.

"But we're here to help out, if you let us," Walls continued.

The guard gave them a look as if he knew that there was something different about them. Then, he said, "Come with me," as he led them in.

10. Speaking to the Queen

The group waited in the healing room which was wide with a glittering window of glass that shone with a bronze light colour in the chamber. The healers wore nurse-like outfits with white robes and a few were wandering around.

The healers used a particular technique: they used the power of the forest to heal their people. For example, they were going to use the pond of extraction as it would take out what was affecting William, healing him totally. But still, LO-NO couldn't accept any of this as he thought it was some mumbo-jumbo stuff.

Floyd and the others sat on a bench against the wall. It felt like they were rejected from a failed school project they had done and were called to wait outside.

"Why have they left us outside?" Walls wondered.

"I THINK THEY WORK BETTER WITHOUT US LOOKING ON." LO-NO said.

"Uh."

"BETTER OFF WITHOUT US."

But still, they left them on edge as they wondered what the guard was doing. He was long gone now, and they had waited for a couple of minutes, but there was no answer for what he was asking them to do.

A healer came over to them and offered them some wet towels. It didn't look as if anyone had used them before: they were clean, refreshing and drippy. Floyd, Walls and Dez took one each and cleaned themselves with it.

"UGH, GROSS!" LO-NO cried out. He didn't know what the towels were for.

As Floyd and the others finished, they passed the towels back to the healer and she walked away.

Then not so long after, Julius came up to them who looked more tense after the experience.

"How is he?" Floyd asked.

"Fine" Julius said quite breathless, "I just wanted to thank you all. I was wrong about you."

"We have our charm" Walls said with a wink.

Julius didn't share any more comments after that as he turned around and headed back to the chamber.

Later another soldier came up to them and instructed, "You should come with me."

The four didn't say much as they got up from the bench and began leaving the chamber.

They journeyed through the streets of the city as people went about their day, noticing the unusual band of outsiders. The people all noticed that they hadn't seen anyone wearing that weird get up, specially the one with so much mechanical body armour.

They made their way up to the tower which seemed to be the beacon of the whole kingdom. It was lean; tall with stairs leading all around it with people going up and down from it. The people who came from this tower were royal members, servants, you name it.

As they reached the top, they arrived in an outdoor environment where they could see the view of the whole city and the forest. It was strange to look at: it appeared that you were looking at two completely different worlds all together.

Then, they spotted stairs leading up to another chamber where there was a young woman with black hair on the left side and white hair on the right. She shone with a glittery dress and had light blue eyes. She also wore a golden crown on her head, which was small with tiny green jewels inside.

Floyd thought he was dreaming, and he noticed that the same effect was happening to Dez and Walls as well. The young woman gave out an enchanted feel whenever you were around her, like something mythical surrounded her.

She glared at the outsiders as she spoke firmly, "I am Queen Mela. What brings you here?"

The four stood there as they didn't have an answer. But Floyd spoke first, "We all came here by accident, your highness. I came here to rescue these two", Floyd looked at Dez and Walls, "and while visiting, I discovered much about what has happened to your world and what you have been going through."

The queen made a very light smile as she glared at them. "So, you know about our history?"

The four nodded as Mela went on, "My ancestors only wanted to communicate with the forest. We knew that we sensed the life all around us. We had an idea, that we could try to speak with it by using the Harness Seed."

"The Harness Seed?" Floyd interrupted, which he didn't mean to.

"Yes. The seed which we've created. Which now everyone blames the royal family for all the destruction it has brought upon us. I know I live within a family of destroyers."

The very thought tumbled her with sorrow, as if nothing could change those events. But Floyd noticed the baggage she carried around her, as he replied, "But there had to be something that you might've miscalculated?"

Mela beamed at the librarian, who continued, "I imagine that you were on a similar page that you were going for, but you might've accidently created something else."

The way this man was speaking, Mela thought, sounded like he had high intelligence, which made her give him much attention.

"You seem to know what you're speaking about," she said.

"Well, I passed a lot of my exams," Floyd said, which didn't change Mela's thoughts. If he knew that something went wrong with the seed, couldn't it be undone?

Then, she hesitated, then said, "Come with me."

The Queen led them through the chamber up the stairs as they followed along. They soon entered a hexagonal room that had an indoor river with grass spiralling all around with bugs hovering over it.

They looked all around the chamber as everything was so lifeful and wonderous.

"For some time, this room has been slowly regenerating the power of life itself, everything growing and moving on as it should be," Mela explained. "There's something here that my people have no awareness of: there is another Harness Seed."

The four looked at her quite blank, "I'm sorry?" Floyd said.

"This room has power from it", the queen went on, "there's no glitches or side effects, everything is responding as I wish it should." Then thoughts clouded her.

"But I don't want to interject here, but why tell us, rather than let everyone know of this?" Dez shared his point.

"It has only been few years now that this one was made. We've checked that everything should go right as planned, but it needs more time to charge."

Then Mela looked at Floyd, "but you on the other hand, seem have the knowledge with quite high intelligence. Maybe you can identify what we did wrong?"

As much as Floyd was intrigued about what the queen was proposing, he didn't understand this type of science. It was way out of his expertise, and it was very unnatural.

"Believe me, your highness," he said, "I can help as I can try, but from what I have gathered already about your planet and what you do, it might be way out of my zone."

Then the queen gave a sharrow look of disappointment. "I thought by the way you speak, maybe you could be someone who could correct our mistake. But it appears not to be."

The four stood there as they thought for the very first time on their quest, they had nothing to do.

"So, is that it then?" Walls said cluelessly, "Mission accomplished?"

"WELL, THAT WAS AN OVERALL POINTLESS TRIP", LO-NO expressed his emotions.

"That isn't the reason why I brought you here", Mela mentioned, as she was slowly changing the subject. "We've been sent a message by another outsider."

The news troubled Floyd, as he didn't know what it might bring. But if it was who Floyd and LO-NO may think it was, the universe might become much smaller for them to fit in.

"This man demands that we hand over someone known by the same descriptions as you", she looked at Floyd. "I have never received a message from anyone outside these walls demanding such a big request- why is that?"

Floyd gave an awkward look as he didn't know what to say.

"Does Frick know who I am?" he thought panicked.

Mela stared at him as she sensed something was off with him. "I can take it that you have some sort of relationship with this man?"

"Uh…No!" Floyd burst out.

"YES, HE REALLY HASN'T!!!", LO-NO defended Floyd, which was something he had never done before.

"So what should I tell him, hmm?" Mela questioned. "Shall I formally tell him of your presence? Only because I don't know what the outside has for me and my people, but I know different civilisations have evolved more than us, and I will give anything to protect my kingdom."

"Then trust me!" Floyd said, but he didn't mean it to sound like that. "You can't give me up to him!"

"And why is that?"

"Because whatever you know about him or the outside world, I'm more valuable. I have the knowledge that could end your world in a blink. If you give me to him, Damola wouldn't be the only world that would be gone forever."

The way Floyd said it told Mela that he was serious. Not knowing much of the universe, Mela couldn't make out what was there and who their invaders were. But she didn't trust any of them if one dared to threaten her kingdom. But she listened to what Floyd said, and it seemed like he was warning her.

Like earlier, this mysterious stranger spoke things quite knowledgeable as if he had experience of every fact he knew. There was something more to this man than she could ever guess.

"I have no intention to make any agreement yet," Mela promised. "But I want you to promise one thing: do not tell anyone about this second seed."

"And you won't give me to Frick: got it," Floyd promised. "But I have to say, we both have quite dangerous outcomes."

The queen walked away as she headed over to the other side of the chamber, while Floyd turned to his pals as they gave a somewhat horrified look. "What are we going to do, Floyd?!" Dez asked him.

"YEAH, WHAT ARE WE REALLY GOING TO DO?!" LO-NO agreed.

"If Frick knows who I am, then we're all in big trouble," Floyd said, as this sounded dire. "There's only one thing that we can do…"

"And what's that?" Walls wondered.

"We'll fight!"

11.   The Upcoming Battle

Earn Frick sat at his desk in his room as he planned to hire certain bounty hunters who may be interested to collect the librarian. He knew through all the years Frick had lived, there was no better prize or award than this! This was the one! The one that every thief, smuggler or whatever would want to make them gods.

A hooded man went into the chamber as he had some news to deliver.

"Frick," he said, as he was a spy, a really good spy Frick paid a while back. "I have updates on the librarian."

A greedy and snarly smile swept across Frick's face.

"Where is he?"

The spy returned with a nudge as his head shied away, trying not to look at him.

"Well? Speak up!"

"He was located in the Kingdom of Larne."

"The Kingdom of Larne," Frick thought, deep in memory about the Kingdom. "Well, we shall get someone to drop in and pick him up."

"Uhh, there's going to be a slight issue with that," the spy added. "The queen has organised to keep him under protection from our hands."

It left Frick in an annoyance that someone who had massive defences would protect such a thing. Queen Mela had sworn to protect the librarian at all costs, which appeared to disturb Frick's plans.

"Hasn't she reconsidered any alternative agreements?" he added.

"No, she stands by her word."

Then Frick had to reorganise himself. "Okay, okay. How are we going to do this, eh?" He narrowed his eyes on the spy.

"Maybe we could…"

"Ah!" Frick pointed a finger out to stop the spy from talking. He was in deep thought, brainstorming ideas in five seconds, which stretched to possibilities that he knew would succeed.

"I want you to send an army of my hired men, including the ones with larger groups, to invade and attack the kingdom…"

"But Boss! You're asking them to go to war with an entire royal army and we may not stand a chance…"

Frick returned an angry stare which frightened the spy.

"Alrighty!" the spy agreed. "I'll call them right away!"

Floyd, Dez and Walls wandered across the street where they observed the artistry of the place. The place looked chilled and quite light, but nothing really zinged. They thought they would take an overall stroll as they lay low. They passed near a garden where they smelt the living air flowing into their noses.

LO-NO was busy getting some food and supplies from the markets and Queen Mela was busy with royal duties. The only pals Floyd could hang out with was still Dez and Walls, who he still had a hard time getting to know.

"So, you think staying here is just a good idea?" Walls asked the question.

"I don't know, man, its all nice and pretty and stuff, but I'm really aching to get back out there," Dez said.

"You mean, back to the stars?" Floyd asked.

"That's right, man!" Dez commented. "It has been some time since we travelled."

"If I may be so bold, how long have you been stranded here?"

Dez and Walls had a rough memory as it seemed so long ago, "Five months?" Walls guessed, "but who knows, when you are trapped under a hole with so many hours to waste, you don't even know what the date is."

Every time Floyd heard a word out of these guys, he seemed to get along with them very well. He knew that they were different than his other friends but there was something about them; he just loved their presence.

Then it left Floyd thinking again, about the letter, as it seemed like he almost had nearly all the questions answered. But yet again, something was more off.

He took it out from his robe's pocket as he held it to them. "Do either of you have any knowledge about what this is?"

The two observed it as they unfolded it and read the whole paper. Then Dez made a bubbling chuckle as he added, "Dude! That's Walls' writing!"

"Why is it so old?"

"It was stored in my library in the future," Floyd explained. "The reason why I came here in the first place is because of this. For some reason, you must've written to give me a heads up about these events."

"So, you're saying that we give you this?" Walls wondered.

Floyd had no right answer. He couldn't tell either he, Dez, Walls, LO-NO or whoever Floyd knew left it in the library, but there was still something unclicking here.

Then, strolling through the street came Mela with a bunch of her royal guards besides her, like they were in defence mode. "Floyd! Frick has returned a message and said that he is going to attack our kingdom!"

This shook them, but it was no surprise that this was going to be the direction Frick headed towards. Floyd froze in motion as he couldn't believe what he had heard that this man was going all extreme, because of him.

"He is not stupidly thinking to fight against an entire royal army, is he?" Floyd had to express.

"Yes, he would" Mela answered.

Floyd shrugged off his fears as he needed to stay in focus. "Do you know when it will happen?"

"Tomorrow at sunrise," Mala reported. "It only leaves a couple of hours for the preparations. I shall begin making plans with the Council."

"Then, I won't take much time off your hand, Your Highness," Floyd replied, as Mela went with her guards to begin making plans.

Floyd on the other hand led Dez and Walls through the street.

"Floyd, you think staying here is a good idea?" Walls asked again.

"Nope, but wherever I go, Frick will follow," Floyd explained, as he knew it would be truly impossible to escape.

"But can't you, 'ZIIIIIIIP!' into another time or what?" Dez asked.

"No, no, I don't want risk getting caught between the time rift."

"Huh?" Walls and Dez commented together.

"If I mess going about into different times and get caught into them, I might lose myself and travel outside of it. Lost forever."

"Sounds very terrifying" Walls thought.

"Point taken," Dez commented. Then he soon picked up, "Hey, where are we going?"

"We're going into battle, gentlemen. We have got to be prepared!"

The thing about training was that you needed to build up a bit of muscle, which don't come up in just a matter of hours. Floyd, Dez and Walls went into a training room where someone taught them simple fighting skills that can come in handy.

They wore Dercan armour and they had a choice of weapons. This trainer was one of the best teachers they could ask for as they said they needed to learn everything that could help them tomorrow, which was asking a lot.

With time passing by, they trained as night fell. The trainer told them everything that they should and shouldn't do, but with as much effort they tried, they were possibly overdoing it.

During the training, they did make a few mistakes where they made a mess across the training room. Even watching them doing their extreme best, it made the other trainers felt awkward.

Floyd nodded to their trainer as they may need a moment. The trainer nodded as Floyd was alone with his friends in the room

"Come on guys," he said with a bit of empathy, "they're about to be here shortly and trash everything."

"We're trying our best", Dez commented as he noticed Walls' helmet was on fire. "Oh, uh, you got a bit of…"

"Bird stuff?" Walls guessed.

"No, no", Dez said carefully.

As Walls noticed the issue and as he put it out, Floyd gave a slow sigh and said honestly, "Look, I wish we had been training for this moment months ago, but time is on the edge and Frick is going knocking on our doors at sunrise."

"Then we'll show him a piece of this!" Walls said drawing a weapon out of its socket.

"Walls, no!" Floyd told him to put it down, which Walls slowly did.

"Sorry," he expressed his apology.

Then, on the other side of the room coming in was LO-NO, who brought a bag of food and supplies with him. Floyd walked up to him while Dez and Walls were cleaning up.

The robot gave a concerned look. "YOU THINK THIS IS WISE?" he asked as if they appeared to be a bad sign.

"What else am I supposed to do?' Floyd told him back. "We've only got one shot of this, or it'll be over."

"WELL, BY THE WAY OF HOW THINGS ARE GOING DOWN, I THINK WE SHOULD BE BETTER TO GET OUT OF HERE WHILE WE HAVE THE CHANCE".

"No", Floyd disagreed as he wouldn't give up. "if we lock ourselves and stay in the library for eternity, Frick will never stop looking for us."

"IT DOESN'T SOUND LIKE A BAD IDEA TO ME".

Floyd tried to figure out another plan as he added, "There has to be a diversion, a master plan we could set up if all else fails." Then he looked straight at LO-NO and thought, "You could be our diversion!"

"WAIT, ME? NO!" the robot burst out. "YOU THINK OF ME PLANNING AHEAD AND THINK OF AN ALTERINTIVE OUTCOME IF THINGS BECOME DIRE?"

"LO-NO, you could be humanity's last chance," Floyd sparked his mind, which the robot didn't like.

"YOU SAID IT LIKE I'M GOING TO BE THE LAST THING WHO STILL MAKES IT IN THE END".

"Well, I'm not going to last forever, am I?" Floyd teased him.

Then LO-NO gave in, "ALRIGHT, FINE. ONLY BECAUSE YOU SAID SO".

Frick was left alone in the laboratory in the late night, as almost all the preparations were nearly complete.

Then came professor Nicator with all the paperwork in his hand as he entered the chamber.

Frick didn't turn around as he asked, "I take it, it is complete?"

"It should take off whenever we make our arrival," Nicator answered, then a worried thought came after. "You think this is wise? What will it cos…"

"Don't," Frick stopped him before Nicator could answer. "I've dreamt this all of my life and now I'm not losing it, even by one man."

The professor quietened down and never said another word.

Frick gazed up through the curtains to what would be used for the upcoming arrival. Then he said, "I would strongly suggest taking any scientist who would be willing to go with you. You are set free; you do not matter to me anymore."

With a confused look Frick explained, "I expect where I will be going, there will be no returning."

Then before Nicator could make his leave, he wanted to share his grateful assistance to Frick, for how useful he had become.

"Thank you" he said as he left.

Mila returned to the chamber where the Harness Seed was. She stared down under the river where it was contained in a bubble shape. She stared at it for a time as she knew it was perfectly safe and secure.

She had no idea what tomorrow may hold, and whoever she was protecting was worth saving. But if Floyd was saying the truth, if Frick got his hands on him, and if anything happened to the second seed, then everything would end.

She had to be curious, for whatever happened tomorrow, she would fight for it. She turned around as she headed back to the door and closed the chamber behind her.

12. Winner takes All

Just before dawn rose, hundreds of Dercans soldiers stood above the gate as they gazed through the forest. They all waited as they couldn't tell when the enemy forces would arrive.

During this time, Floyd was asleep after being exhausted from all the hard training he had been through. He tried to force himself to get up when it was all happening, but he didn't have the strength to do so.

Meanwhile, Dez and Walls were waiting for their librarian friend as they stood in the front line. Curiously, Walls asked Dez, "Isn't he meant to be here?"

Dez returned an unknowing look as he shrugged. "Beats me, dude. When do you think it's going to start?"

Walls had no idea. They waited for about an hour and nothing had sparked their attention. None of the soldiers said when Frick's men were going to attack, and the people stayed in their homes or went to some other areas in the kingdom for protection.

They waited for some time as the duo thought they could waste the time. They played a game while flicking some pebbles and tossed them as far as they would go, and began doing some beat boxing.

A few minutes passed and then they saw in the distance was a spaceship. A large spaceship that grew hundreds of feet as it got closer and was quite tall. The soldiers stood on guard as they braced in position.

But then, something worse alerted them: more spaceships, not as massive, zoomed from other directions heading head towards them.

The Dercans didn't have weapons that could blast their enemies out of the sky; they knew they would be out-gunned, so the only way for them to attack was to wait till they landed.

The spaceships landed in a few basements of the city as crowds of henchmen with body armour carried blasters in their arm as the Dercans charged and fought. Then, massive numbers of so many of the two forces crowed like a party but everyone was fighting.

A few of the ships in the air flew across. The Dercans noticed that Frick was playing a bigger game and knew who the prize was. A bunch of his men avoided any contact with the soldiers as they searched for the librarian. They looked in buildings, objects, or at maps.

Walls and Dez were in the middle of it all as they watched the battle unfold in front of them. They were a bit far apart of it all as they thought they may not be entirely useful in this scenario.

"We were wrong about this, weren't we?" Dez asked Walls, regretting.

"We so were!" Walls agreed. "Quick! Let's find a quieter location so nobody will find us!"

"Good call!" Dez gave a thump up as they started to run.

It was only a massive rumble from a blast which woke Floyd. He noticed the big explosion from the garden outside of his room which was dishevelled. Floyd was shocked that he had slept in as he hurried to put on his gear.

After a couple of seconds of wearing the armour, and holding a spear, the librarian burst through his door as he made way towards one of the nearby streets where a band of soldiers marched their way.

But behind him, he noticed that he wasn't alone, and someone was trying to catch up.

"FLOYD!" said the voice of LO-NO. "YOU'RE A LIBRARIAN! NOT A SOLDIER!!!!"

"Buzz off, LO-NO!" Floyd told him off as he tried not to sound so rude; he was in a rush, and he knew he had to help out. But Floyd wasn't thinking straight at that moment, LO-NO was right, he wasn't a soldier; he wasn't trained to be a soldier throughout his life, but knew he was in a battle for the fight of his life, and possibly for the rest of existence.

He knew if Frick got what he wanted, Floyd wouldn't know what sort of chaos he might inhabit. Another Hollow disaster? Meddling with time? Destroying all of humanity's knowledge and making the library his own new castle?! That last one worried Floyd the most.

Overall, as LO-NO did state as a last result, they could always leave anytime, but Floyd couldn't. He had to put up a stand against Frick and that was going to be today!

The battle continued as it brawled all over the place. The people still kept safe in the areas that they were located as they heard the sounds of battle. Meanwhile, Dez and Walls were still running as they saw a few areas of the battles were taking place close to them.

They tried to run through the corridors with the tall walls but they seemed to get stuck. They wrenched their heads about as they knew they had nowhere to go.

"Man, this is hopeless," Walls commented.

"No, we have to fight our way out of this!" Dez said as he took out his weapon again. "If there's one thing that we learnt about all this, is that Floyd is the one we can trust."

"Yeah!" Walls agreed as he took out his own weapon. "For Floyd! And to the very things that we tried to accomplish in our lives but failed them on a number of accounts."

"That's the right attitude!" the duo looked in one direction as they took a deep breath.

Before they charged, Floyd popped right in as he spotted the duo and ran towards them.

"There you are!" Floyd called in relief.

"Where have you been?" Dez wondered.

"Slept in," the librarian revealed the truth. "Had a very rough night."

"Same," Walls agreed as they noticed that the fighters were drawing closer to them. "So, what should we do? Fight them off? Hide?"

"Beats me," the librarian gave in. "I have never accepted something so beyond my wits. I've delt with reality destroying itself, saving humanity. But fighting in a warzone is not my strong point."

Even as Floyd looked at it, he knew they wouldn't stand a chance if they tried. They were no fighters.

And then, to everyone surprise, the sky above started to change colour. With a shocking red gloom they watched the clouds simmer and wither. And a massive rocket hovered above the kingdom with a spiral ring thrusting in speed around it.

They watched in horror as they had no idea what it was. Even Floyd had no understanding of what it could do.

"That's Frick's secret weapon?!" Walls thought with a shocked expression.

"If Frick is going to use it, we may not survive any of it!" Dez mentioned as he was quickly deciding that they should run.

But all the soldiers just froze, knowing that it would be pointless to keep fighting on if the risk was too high. But this was Floyd's choice, and he was determined about what he was going to do.

"STTTTOOOOPPPPP!!!!!!", he called out to the crowed as he walked forward. Walls and Dez watched him go without joining him. "Tell your boss that he has got what he asked for; I volunteer to go."

13.   Final Preparations

By how things were going now, chances were grim. Frick had total control of everything under his fingers, which the Dercans could do nothing about but were forced to stand down.

The troops did nothing as they couldn't make a signal or anything as it would have triggered Frick's men. While everyone else stayed where they had been in the last hour, they waited until the Queen gave the all-clear sign.

Floyd journeyed up to the tower and entered a meeting room with Mela and Earn. While Earn was busy talking, he was nevertheless pleased that he finally got what he came for.

"I sure do thank you for making the agreement," Frick said.

"I only stood down because you have threatened my Kingdom," Mela returned a look, thinking that Frick had won too easily. "This isn't over."

"Oh, my dear, I had already won before you started to realize that all of your power cannot harm me."

Mela knew this was unfair; all of Frick's abilities and toys, all the things that he and his crew had accomplished, was only for his gain. Mela still believed she had made a deal with someone who wanted to take some else.

"You can't own someone. He has more of a life like everyone else alive."

"But he is more important than that," Frick explained. "This is a man from the future, the last man of mankind."

Mela stared at Floyd with a look of shock, and Floyd tried to hide away to not make eye contact.

"He shall teach me everything and show me everything." Frick went on. "I'll be the one who will know everything and what shall happen and no one else will have that knowledge."

Mela glared at Frick, as she had to come to terms that Floyd was in fact was telling the truth. She had failed, not knowing what Frick may do now.

"But you know meddling with things beyond your abilities will bring consequences," Mela tried to plead. "I have learnt the responsibility to not follow the same mistakes that my family have made. You can't just simply do what you feel like."

A few of Frick's men moved but Frick put his hand up as a sign to not intervene. "I've gone further than what anyone has done," Frick said, serious. "I will declare everything in my will, and no one will question it."

Floyd gave a startled wave to Frick as he tried to get some attention. "I'm sorry to barge in like this, but she has a very important point," the librarian said, while choosing his words carefully. "You might destroy branches of events or ripple the time continuum."

"I am very aware of the risk," Frick said casually, "but I'm more interested in where you're at with things." Then, he gave the sign for them to leave: as he got up, he said "Come Floyd, we've got much to discuss."

But before they left, Frick turn to Mela as he added one last thing, "And just so you know; I will push the trigger if you do in fact break our agreement."

Then they walked through the doors and exited the room, with the Queen left alone, not knowing what may happen next.

One of her loyal servants came to her seat as he asked, "You're not seriously considering letting this man walk away with it?"

"I'm afraid he has." Mela said doubtful, "Call our troops in."

"Then what about the people? What will they know about these events?"

"They must not know, as this is forbidden knowledge, even by our creators."

Then, Mela made her way out of the chamber and she started heading to where the Harness Seed was.

The soldiers were called back to base as they marched through the streets. All of Frick's henchmen stood watching as they kept patrol of every sector of the Kingdom.

LO-NO snuck through their attention as he passed from building to building, hoping to find the only people he knew could help him now. He had briefly heard that Floyd had surrendered himself, which was typical LO-NO thought. And Frick was about to take off in an hour, which wasn't long to make an escape plan.

He headed towards their cabin house where they had been staying.

LO-NO knocked to try to get a response, "HEY, ITS ME!", the robot said quietly, "OPEN UP! WE GOT TO TALK RIGHT NOW!!"

Nothing returned, then a very brief voice replied, "Go away." That was, of course, Walls.

LO-NO shrugged, not because of disbelief but annoyance. "THEY'VE CAPTURED FLOYD AND WE ARE RUNNING OUT OF TIME BEFORE THINGS REALLY GET A BAD TURN!"

By the way LO-NO expressed it, it forced the terror out of the duo as they opened the door and let the robot in. The room was darkened and cramped as they tried to make very little light so no one would know they were there.

LO-NO turned to the duo who had taken off their pieces of armour and looked wrecked.

"BY THE WAY", LO-NO added, "I DON'T BUY THIS STORY YOU HAVE BEEN SAYING WHO YOU ARE".

"Well, we don't believe you're a robot," Dez burst back. Then he and Walls observed the robot's appearance and returned, "No, maybe you are what you say you are."

LO-NO shrugged again as he knew that they were wasting time by the moment. "OKAY, WE'VE GOT TO FIND A WAY TO SNEAK ON BOARD WITHOUT ANYONE NOTICING."

The three brainstormed some ideas which could work. Walls and Dez came up with something, "Maybe if we go in, we could join Frick and his crew and say we'll be his pawns," Walls thought.

"UH, THAT'S NOT…"

"And we can make a diversion that allow you, YO-NO…" Dez followed on.

"ACTUALLY, THAT'S NOT MY NA…".

"So, you could shut everything down in the rocket and KA-BLAM! We set free Floyd, take down Earn Frick and live happily ever after," Walls concluded as the duo hi-fived each other.

Then it made LO-NO reconsider, "ACTUALLY, THAT'S NOT A BAD PLAN," he thought. "BUT I DON'T THINK JUST THE THREE OF US COULD BE ENOUGH."

"Of course we are," Walls said quite positive, "we don't need a bunch of people just to take on an entire army."

"THAT'S EXCATLLY WHAT WE'RE FACING".

"But look where that got them."

"So, just by the three of us, we can make this an easy win."

It sounded easy with some complications. It troubled LO-NO more as he thought about it. There was just too much on the line, but he had to admit to himself that there may not be anything else left that may be on the line as well.

"I'M NOT SO SURE ABOUT IT THOUGH", the robot had to say. "THE ODDS ARE STILL PRETTY SLIM."

"Then, what else are we going to do?" Dez asked, as he knew that they didn't have a lot of options.

Then a horrifying thought troubled LO-NO which he was afraid to ask about.

Mela went back to the chamber once again as she spent her time staring down at the seed, guessing whether it would be time or not. With only a matter of…well, she didn't know how long she would have till

Frick started meddling with things. She knew he didn't know what he would unleash.

She stood there while taking notice that someone was in the room with her. She turned around to see the strange shape similar to a man.

"SORRY TO TROUBLE YOU", LO-NO expressed. "I THINK THERE MAY BE ONE THING THAT COULD SAVE ALL OUR LIVES…".

"I wouldn't allow it," Mela stopped him, as she knew what this metal man was speaking about. "If this may be our final chance of bringing Damola back from its ashes, then I can't risk losing it."

"CAN I EXPLAIN BEFORE YOU TELL ME TO GET OUT?"

The Queen listened as she waited to hear what LO-NO had to say.

"WE ONLY HAVE A MATTER OF MOMENTS NOW, AND THERE ISN'T MUCH ANY OF US CAN DO. YOU HAVE HEARD FLOYD…".

"That he has come from the future, yes I did know."

It caught LO-NO off guard as he tried to get back into shape. "THEN YOU KNOW THAT TERRIBLE THINGS COULD YET COME. I'M ONLY ASKING IF THERE'S SOMETHING SPECIAL THAT THIS SEED COULD DO, COULD IT POSSBLY TAKE OUT ANY POWER ON THE ROCKET?'

Mela froze as she tried to think. She noticed the effect it had on their forest, but she didn't know how things worked with these technologies.

"What we have studied, it has a strong energy that strips away from anything that is life, if that means anything," she said, only guessing the science.

"TRUST ME, ANYTHING CAN GO PASSING THROUGH MY HEAD AFTER WHAT I'VE LEARNT HERE."

She did not know what the robot had in mind, but it troubled her the most to let it go. "But how can I trust you with it?" she asked worrying. "What if it falls under the hands of Earn? And he would use it for some bad purposes?"

LO-NO could sense her fears, that she wasn't fully giving the support to LO-NO's plan in anyway, but Floyd had given him a role that he must do, he had no other choice.

"WELL, I MAY NOT BE SURE ON THAT," the robot said. "BUT THE BEST WE CAN DO IS TRY."

14.   Show time!

Frick and his men were ready to take off as they brought the librarian on board the rocket. A wide stairway led to the entrance as a few of Frick's men kept guard in case anything came ahead. With only a few seconds to spare, they thought no one would likely come on board.

But to their surprise, Dez, Walls and LO-NO crept under the ring barrier of the rocket and headed towards a nearby hatch which they realized was locked.

LO-NO took out a tool kit then a small thin tool and laser burned the edges of the hatch. He carefully did it while Walls and Dez watched in worry as they checked that none of Frick's men spotted them.

"How long does that thing take?" Walls asked desperately.

"UNTIL I CAN GET THIS OPEN," the robot replied back as he couldn't lose focus.

"Won't they catch us easily?" Dez asked.

"THAT DOESN'T MATTER," the robot said, not thinking straight. "WELL, NOTHING MATTERS IF WE DON'T END THIS NOW."

LO-NO took his time as the duo noticed some of the henchmen walking quite near to them. They lowered their heads as they tried not to be seen.

Then, the walkway started to fold back in as they guessed that the rocket was soon to take off.

Then, LO-NO got the hatch open as Walls and Dez pulled the door away and they snuck in. Then, they heard the turbines flaring up and a massive gust of wind blew on the service. As they got into the chamber, they saw the rings spinning as the rocket slowly moved up a couple of feet.

Then, with getting on board making it seem so easy, they noticed they were in an empty chamber with no one present so they planned for the next step.

"So, what were we going to do again?" Dez asked, forgetting.

"YOU TWO HAVE TO MAKE A DIVERSION," LO-NO told them. "I GOT MY PART OF THE PLAN SORTED."

"Good call," Walls said as they went over to a door and opened it up. There they were caught in a corridor that split to left and right. Clean, shiny with sleek walls and floor. They went separate ways as they planned to shut this rocket down for good.

Floyd was in a wide circular room with bunch of scientists who sat at their computer panels. The librarian sat at a table in the centre, strapped as a few of the scientists put on these head pieces that were attached to a machine next to him.

The librarian's eyes looked in many different directions, as he had a hard time seeing what was going on around him. The only thing that he could see directly was the bright light above him and Frick looking down at him.

He could hear the scientists typing and making as little noise as possible so as not to interrupt Frick's conversation with Floyd.

"What are they doing?" Floyd asked quite unsure, but part of him didn't want to know what Frick was going to do to him.

Frick gave a subtle smile. "You know if someone knows something, and they don't tell truth…"

"So, a lie detector?" Floyd guessed.

"No, no, no, no," Frick waved his finger. "We're going to scan and learn everything all about you. All of your knowledge, what you have seen and been, almost everything we'll know."

Floyd gave a look of panic as Frick made a cheerful chuckle. "Oh, this is so exciting, isn't it?"

Floyd didn't want to know. He bent to see the scientists as they were working their hardest.

Then another thought popped into his head which made him nervous to think about.

"So, when you do in fact go to the future and have everything, what's your plan for me?"

"Nothing much special," Frick thought, as he hadn't come to full terms with that. "I was going to use you as my own prize, as you are the last man of all existence, but if I'm the last one, I'm not sure if keeping you would be necessary. But yet again, if you have some scientific skills, I could keep you."

"Oh no! I am so useful!" Floyd pleaded. "Ha! You would be surprised by what I had to go through to pass all of my exams for the Last Court. It was a rough few years of my life but worth it!"

Frick gave Floyd a promising narrowing eye as he was liking what the librarian had said. Floyd meanwhile wished he could get out of there, try to make it back to the library and get away from all of this.

Then, something caught their attention as two figures walked up from a door to a corridor. There, Floyd watched in relief but also in confusion; Dez and Walls. The two were wearing two different outfits as they stood out.

Walls wore a glittery white suit with nice black shiny shoes, and a cone hair style; while Dez, on the other hand, looked like a hipster with a sleeveless shirt, some big sneakers and sunglasses.

Frick and most of the scientists stared at them, giving out the same response as Floyd. "Who are these infidels?!" Frick called out as he waited for a response.

"I'm so glad that you have taken notice of us," Walls told Frick with a narrow frown, which Frick didn't know how to response back.

"Hope you love a show," Dez commented. "Because we're going to give a fantastic show for you all!"

There was no action they did in this moment, as Frick wanted them locked up, but he seemed to like them already.

"Sure," he said, as he lay back in his seat. "Let's get some light on them."

There, the whole room went dark except for the computer panels. The light from the top beamed towards Dez and Walls and they knew they were the centre of attention. Then they were off!

LO-NO crept through the corridors and sneakily passed anyone that was coming ahead of him. He shortly made his way to the rocket's core where he arrived in a room with a massive tall pilar with spinning plates on it. The room glowed pure red which gave a feeling of raw radiant power flowing.

Nearby, LO-NO spotted a separate room which had all sorts of science equipment and tech. There was a bunch of wires connecting to many machines that LO-NO didn't have time to identify.

LO-NO pointed at whatever may come in handy as things were getting a bit too confused. Then he spotted a machine that looked like a microwave but appeared to be some sort of scanning device.

LO-NO took out the second Harness Seed from his pouch as he thought this might do the trick. He walked over, put it on a plate and then placed it in the machine. The robot presses a button as some laser scanner was trying to produce the plant but as it did so, something was happening.

Dez and Walls rapped a couple of songs they knew, as they gave it all. Lights flared around with colours as Frick was having a blast watching. Floyd, on the other hand, tried to get out of his straps as he knew this was the perfect time to escape.

"My, why shouldn't I hire some entertainers from earlier?" Frick thought while watching. "These are quite marvellous performers. I wonder where they came from?"

"I wonder the same," Floyd said as he continued to get part of his arms out.

For some mysterious reason, it kept Frick thinking how they would have come with him with so little notice. It seemed quite…in motion. He couldn't put his thought to it, but something kept him questioning.

"It makes me more curious about who they are," Frick said. "What are they? What do they want?"

While the duo continued their performance, some buzzing of electricity flittered around the room as the light flicked on and off. Everyone stood up, off guard, and the observed the room.

"What on Damola is going on?!" Frick called out, demanding answers.

The scientists looked at their screens as one replied, "Something has affected our systems and the whole core!"

"WHAT?!" Frick cried out. "What sort of virus would infect our ship?!"

Floyd could think of numerous possibilities, but none could withstand a powerhouse ship from Frick, except maybe an enchanted seed. Then the ship tilted on one side as everyone fell, including Frick. It got Floyd tilting roughly as one of his arms got loose.

He tried to set himself free until Frick saw what he was doing. Frick rose up and used every part of his body to race toward Floyd. "No!", he yelled, "you will not get away from me! We've got a lot of work to do!"

Then the ship tilted again and Frick fell down on the floor again, and Floyd still had the advantage. Walls and Dez came to his aid as they loosened the straps.

Frick stared up at them, as his energy was weighing him down. "I knew that there was something up with you two," he said very coldly.

But that comment didn't bother them. "Come on!" Dez said as the three started to run. "We've got to get out of here while we still have the chance!"

Then one last voice boomed as they left the chamber. "I will get what you have, Floyd!" this was Frick. "I will know everything!"

The rocket became very unstable, as LO-NO had planned. But that was only a piece of the plan; the main problem now was to get out.

They made their way through corridors as they were stopped by a handful of henchmen, aiming their blasters at them.

"Don't move!", one warned. But before they did something, a heavy rumble shook them as the ship dived down, causing them to slide.

Later Floyd, Dez and Walls ran through the loaming corridor as they tried to find any near escape pods. But the booming and clashing with the ship wasn't helping them.

They tried to hold on to the walls as they slowly marched forward.

"Where did you say LO-NO would be meeting us?" Floyd asked the duo.

"I don't know!" Walls replied. "He didn't give us the full intention of his plan."

"Well, that's just typical LO-NO," Floyd thought as an explosion hit on the other side of the way near them as the air tried to pull them out.

"Don't let go!!!!" Dez said, worrying.

"Wasn't going to, man!!" Walls replied.

The three tried to hold on till they were consumed with it and the very next thing they knew, they were falling to their doom.

As they swung and dived down to the Kingdom, they could see the rocket slowly spinning in a strange direction. Then they heard, BOOOMM!!!! And the whole thing exploded which seriously shocked them, but not as much as the state they were in now.

While they tried to hopefully pray to stay alive for a couple of minutes, something quickly made its way towards them. A small sleek ship with increased speed spotted the trio in danger and it tried its best to save them.

"NOT THIS TIME, FLOYD," LO-NO thought as he got the ship's roof open up and reached towards them. While just making a hundred feet above the ground, the ship swooped them in as they landed clunkily down on a solid floor.

They ached with pain as all their muscles were sore from the fall. They couldn't get up but made movements on the floor instead.

"Owi…" Walls groaned.

Floyd looked at who got them as he sighed in relief, "I thank you for the pickup…".

"NO, I PRETEND THAT THIS WHOLE EXPERINCE NEVER HAPPENED", LO-NO commented as he tried to forget that they had got into trouble while finding a bunch dudes along the way and saved Damola. This was not LO-NO's doing and he refused acknowledge it.

"Man, I can't believe that we blew the Queen's last chance to save her world," Dez commented with sorrow, feeling quite bad about it.

Then LO-NO replied, "I DIDN'T TAKE THE SEED."

Then the three looked blank, "What?!"

"THE QUEEN GAVE ME ANOTHER REPLICA THAT HAD THE SAME INFECTION. I THOUGHT IF I USED THE SAME PATTERN THAT GOT THE FOREST ALL MOPPY, IT MIGHT DO US A LOT OF GOOD DESTORYING FRICK'S ROCKET."

"But why didn't you tell us that?" Floyd wondered.

"I DIDN'T WANT FRICK KNOWING OUR PLAN IF THINGS GOT DESPRATE."

The three didn't question it as LO-NO took them back to the Kingdom where there was a special something the Queen wanted them to attend.

15.   A Fresh New Start

Queen Mela brought all the Dercans - ones in the Kingdom and others hiding in their hatches - to come and gather in this one spot in the forest. And those who had hidden in the trees all this time came along to the Kingdom. This spot was where the last ceremony happened, after so long.

Everyone stood as they watched their Queen standing with the Harness Seed in her hand as she stood towards a tree. This was the tree where they gave the last seed but now they were ready to correct it.

The tension swelled in Mela as troubled thoughts clouded her mind. She closed her eyes as she took a deep breath, letting the air go from the old world and letting in the new. She kneeled down as she planted the seed.

Few seconds passed as the depressed and foggy forest soon glowed green. The grass straightened normally, and new flowers began to appear; green branches sprang up as everything became so full of life again.

Everyone gasped in wonder as some hadn't seen this state of their world in such a very long time. Mela looked around, in such relief and peace as the world they once all knew wasn't now a fairy tale; now everyone will see their beacon.

Elsewhere, across all of Damola, the survivors moved out of their hatches and noticed something was changing. They couldn't believe their eyes for what they were seeing.

Mela knew that it was time for the next step to make new preparations. Now that their barricaded city was no longer needed, they could finally have a fresh start and make more towns and villages.

Everyone was happy, since after a very long time, they could now finally be in peace.

After the ceremony, Floyd, Walls and Dez sat on some nice benches in the forest where everyone was walking about. In spite of all that Floyd had learnt and solved through his recent adventure, there was just something that left him…absent.

The stuff with Dez and Walls, leaving a letter in the library and him not remembering. Floyd knew that there was something up with it but he couldn't shake what.

He was busy playing a small game with them as he drifted off with thought.

"Hey, wasn't I meant to go first?" Walls asked Dez.

"I was yellow!" Dez replied. "By the way, Floyd should get a moment to think on what to do next."

"Good call!" Walls agreed as they looked at the librarian, and noticed he wasn't paying attention. "What's wrong?"

Floyd went back to them as he replied, "Sorry," he expressed as he still couldn't shake the feeling. "From everything that I have done here, I still can't make out how I met you."

That was a question both Dez and Walls couldn't help Floyd with, even though it was so strange and it led them to here.

"But hey, at least we are here, and making the best memories out of it," Walls added, trying not to make Floyd feel bad.

"Yeah, well, it doesn't matter right now, doesn't it?" Floyd agreed as he tried to cheer up.

Floyd knew inside that he may never find out, then one last thing dropped into his mind as he thought to asked Dez and Walls, "Who were the people who were bothering us, again?"

The two tried to gain the memories through their heads, as Dez remembered, "I think they came from Tarmis. Part of the Gaol Government. I couldn't tell what they're drift was but they seemed interested in meeting you for some reason."

A tingle flowed through Floyd as another feeling passed inside him. He thought whatever he happened to him must've led him to them. Floyd only knew very small things about the Gaols as they were secretive, but possibly one day he would get the answers.

But now, Floyd was just glad he was here, saving another society from doom, putting an end to a whole pollution of crime, and just learning that you may get more surprises in the universe than you think you know.

THE END

Appendix

Liam the Author

This Appendix is included for those who are interested in how Liam became an author and how he develops his ideas. Liam hopes that this can create understanding that people with his disabilities can have great things to say and share with the world. Liam also hopes that all those who share his disabilities and want to write can hopefully benefit from learning about how he does it.

Liam often starts with notes for a story, but finds handwriting much more difficult than two-finger typing. He then brainstorms an outline of ideas for the plot.

When he writes the actual story he just doesn't stop till its done, usually within a few weeks. When Liam started his business in August 2022, he had written the base stories of around 10 stories which he is gradually editing and printing. (Now he has added about four more).

After the base story is done, Liam takes his time to come back in to do edits of the story and try to improve his spelling and grammar as best he can. This can take quite a while. When he is happy with it, he hands on to his mum to edit for spelling and grammar that he has not been able to do.

His mum tries to keep Liam's own way with words as much as possible – hence the books are not like professionally edited books, and his mum is not perfect either! The books are the proud work of her son with disability, so she does not want to detract from the authenticity of that, while still making them readable to others. She then hands back to Liam so he can correct anything she has misunderstood. Sometimes they have discussions during editing to work out what Liam actually meant and how to best say it. When Liam is happy, his mum does a final read, correcting any outstanding errors she can find, and its ready for printing.

Before Liam could read and write, (which was not till late in his teen years), but as soon as he could hold a crayon, Liam was prolific with his storytelling using pictures. Generally, these were long comic-strip-type stories. An example of this is the final attachment. Liam has folders and folders of these picture stories.

Original Outline for The Cursed Planet

Below is Liam's original brainstorm/outline for The Cursed Planet, which contains all major plot and character ideas.

ENCHANTRESS FOREST

Walls have purple hair with headphones and a stick out jacket with a stripy shirt.

Dez has long blond hair with a colourful shirt. He likes making money and sharing it with Dez.

Hatches: On the wispery and foggy forest of the dead, hidden metel underground bases have suriovers of the forest. Some suveiors are out there (or were). as dangous beasts lurk around and hunt for any creatures.
Meanwhile a light and crustal kingdom has a best defence in the world, but he may not incousnate with anyone, or treatiors.
One charter can tell who the person is with a touch, Blue skin with pony tails with silver eyes.

The Adventures on Damola:
- Castle
- Crash landed, ruin Giant Stgues.
- Forest, Hatch (Dez and Walls)
- Spooky Forest and Cruse Stauge.
- Ruin Village
- Trible woods?
- Good Castle

Act 1: crime lord Earn have been taking his rules across the galaxy as he try to become the most richest man in the galaxy as he lives in his castle on Damola. Meanwhile, Floyd has been making a life for himself as he tries both going on adventures and returning back to the Library.

Plot Point 1: while cleaning up on the library, Floyd gets a email from LO-NO as Floyd had no memory of these strangers. Floyd and LO-NO make their way on the Osram Star where they met Floyd's old pal John as he takes them to a star gazer junkie as he told them where they are and Floyd gives him some cash for a vechle. While LO-NO and Floyd crash landed on Damo, they arrive on a creepy and mysertous forest where they find destroy villages as monsters lurk

Act 2: as LO-NO and Floyd try to survive in the forest, they step into a metal door hole where they acounter the men who knew Floyd.
They told Floyd and the history about their adventure and they had to force to wipe Floyd's brain, but they have a new trouble as a war between two kingdoms, and a crime lord is playing his cards in between.
Eran wanted take the jawls inside the heart of the silver kingdom as when the evil queen strike as he gets his hand on them.

Plot Point 2: as Floyd and the party make their journey towards the silver kingdom, they make warning for the queen that the evil queen is coming on her way with a massive army as they have to be prepared and a spy is working with her.

Act 3: as the two armies fought in a battle between light and dark, Eran gets his hand on one of the men Floyd didn't knew as he learn about Floyd.
Floyd makes a decision to go to Eran's castle as he wanted to talk to Eran as he has a plan with the queen and the other side to attack Eran.
As Eran's castle gets attacked, the army attacks as Eran's ship try to escape with Floyd as the army take on the sky. Uion joins the battle to only get suck out of space from Floyd.

Climax: as the battle was over, Eran's ship get crash on the forest as Eran makes his way in the deadly forest as he has no longer have control with his castle, his business or anything.
The Queen try to think of a resourceful action to the other side and try to make the world what it used to be, as for Floyd, he just take his new friends out of there and headed back into the cosmos.

In the begging, Eran hired a group of men to hist a ship with a lot of gold.

Example of Liam's unedited writing

A portion of Chapter 2 is reproduced here in Liam's words written as best as he can, before his mum edits.

2) The Curious Letter

Elsewhere, in the far future, a library, in shape of a cube hovered into the blackness of nothingness that holds the many knowledge and history of humanity and everything that ever happened in the universe before its dismissal end.

In the library had two robots who were busy packing some old boxes of their belongings that they didn't knew was theirs, including the librarian who did returned after his missing appsent. When he returned, he promised to give out his robots some noticed on where he would be going, by using these time traveling transmats.

The robots did the head start just before the librarian, Floyd magically appear in thin air as parcels beam around him. Floyd looked like he seemed like he came back from some sort of party as flairs of colour were on his red robe.

LO-NO looked to the librarian as he asked, "WHERE WERE YOU IN THE LAST FORTY-EIGHT HOURS?".

"it was the semi-finals", Floyd explained as he took noticed of the carboard boxes.

You propply think that the boxes were stored from the ceiling, but with a moveable flying cube library drifting into the abyss, the boxes came from an aera inside of the library called the Honex.

The location of the Honex lay underneath in one part of the library's bookshelves against the wall, where pass behind it led down a creepy stairwell that you didn't knew existed. Down at the bottom lay a wooden door that had a soiled golden nob.

After turning the nob, on the other side of the door lay giant gears platform that function the library. the gears speed were different as some spet the same level as each other as some just stop at one point, then sometimes they move backwards with mighty spccd.

They know the builders did a mecsifent job by all of this, from the details of the rooms and chambers, to making across platforms a challenge.

But after you make your way across them carefully, you could find the carboard boxes on the other side, stacking there for quite some time.

Floyd studied at the boxes as he asked, "what's all this?".

"AH, WE FOUND THEM IN THAT CHAMBER DOWN BELOW WHERE THE LIBRARIANS INSTRUCT US NOT TO MEDDLE WITH".

"I think we've gone a bit overboard then meddling", the librarian commented as he walked over to one of the boxes as he opened it. the sort of items he took out were at random at best. There were bunch of notebooks, some were from the `Last Court of the Loyal Librarians, there were some fancy displays, including a hawi doll and a hat. A hat that Floyd never knew exist, it was like a country like hat as he observes it, but he didn't try it on.

As he scowls through the box, Floyd asked the robots, "what made you wanted to check out all of this random stuff?".

"WE WERE JUST CERIOUS ON WHAT THEY'RE STORY IS", LO-NO told the librarian, "YOU KNOW THAT THEY'VE HAVEN'T BEEN OPENED FOR CENTRIES AND EVERYONE JUST FORGOT ABOUT THEM?".

"and they've just been sitting down there all this time?", Floyd though it was quite odd. More unpercuiler at most, "hmmm", he could only say.

Later as Floyd's hand pick out a certain something he touches. An emplhpope, a really old one in fact. it had the exact red pin on it in the front that people don't do in meillina ago.

Floyd was beaming and folded it around in different direction, meanwhile YO-NO was running into the boxes as his brother yelled at him, which the fixing components wasn't solved yet.

Then, Floyd noticed on the letter had a fage name on it, as it suspired him on what it says on it. "huh?", he said as he knew that name was not mistaken than…*Floyd.*

Floyd opened up the letter as he read:

Yo, Floyd, You

I know this must be really weird for you reading this but we've met.

Sort of.

Sorry, we wish we could explain everything, but we could only write one letter.

The main thing you need to know is we're in trouble, and I mean big trouble.

And what we only know by our brief encounter, we need your help, and bring whatever help you have on you, we REALLY need it!

We are located on the planet, Damola.

From us, Dez and Walls

Liam telling his stories through cartoons

(before he could use words well enough to write)

Liam drew pictures from an early age, setting out his stories in his comic form, often divided into chapters. He was prolific in his comic-story drawing all through his childhood. Below is one example of his cartooning.

www.ingramcontent.com/pod-product-compliance
Lightning Source LLC
Chambersburg PA
CBHW061105100726
47911CB00012B/398